WOLF & PARCHMENT

VOL. 1

NEW THEORY SPICE & WOLF

BY ISUNA HASEKURA

ILLUSTRATED BY JYUU AYAKURA

THE YOUNG MAN
ASPIRING TO BE A PRIEST
COL

"YES, REALLY, SO PLEASE
CALM DOWN—"
YOUR EARS AND TAIL
ARE STICKING OUT!

THE DAUGHTER OF A
WOLF AND A MERCHANT
MYURI

IGNORING ALL THE SCREAMING IN HIS HEART,
MYURI OPENED HER EYES WIDE AND GRINNED
WITH SATISFACTION, PULLING HIM INTO A HUG
LIKE A WOLF DEVOURING ITS PREY.

"I LOVE YOU, BROTHER! THANK YOU!"

THE BEAST'S TAIL THAT WAS THE SAME COLOR AS HER HAIR
SWISHED BACK AND FORTH QUITE ENTHUSIASTICALLY,
BETRAYING HER TREMENDOUS DELIGHT.

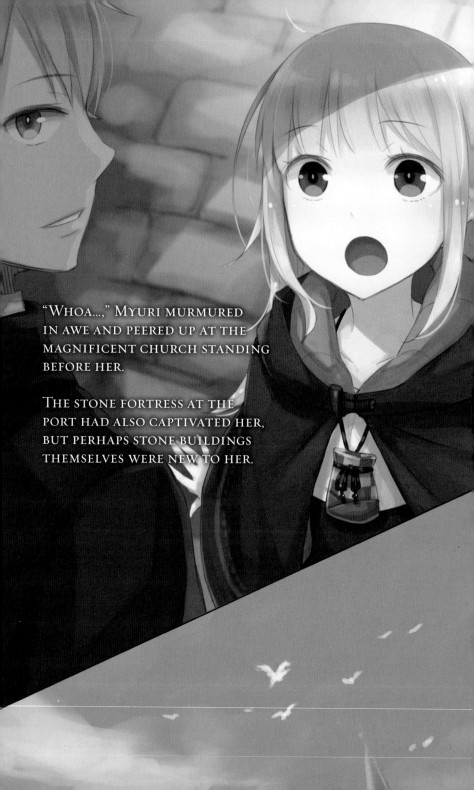

"Whoa...," Myuri murmured in awe and peered up at the magnificent church standing before her.

The stone fortress at the port had also captivated her, but perhaps stone buildings themselves were new to her.

DIRECTOR OF THE
DEBAU COMPANY
TRADING HOUSE
STEFAN

IT WAS HYLAND HIMSELF.
"MY, HEIR HYLAND."

"AND YOU HAVE NOT
CHANGED, SAGE COL."

HEIR TO THE
WINFIEL KINGDOM
HYLAND

Contents

WOLF & PARCHMENT

❧ NEW THEORY SPICE & WOLF ❧

VOL. 1

ISUNA HASEKURA

JYUU AYAKURA

YEN ON

NEW YORK

WOLF & PARCHMENT, Volume 1
ISUNA HASEKURA

Translation by Jasmine Bernhardt
Cover art by Jyuu Ayakura

This book is a work of fiction. Names, characters, places, and incidents are the product of the author's imagination or are used fictitiously. Any resemblance to actual events, locales, or persons, living or dead, is coincidental.

Yen On
1290 Avenue of the Americas
New York, NY 10104

Visit us at yenpress.com
facebook.com/yenpress
twitter.com/yenpress
yenpress.tumblr.com
instagram.com/yenpress

First Yen On Edition: November 2017

Yen On is an imprint of Yen Press, LLC.
The Yen On name and logo are trademarks of Yen Press, LLC.

The publisher is not responsible for websites (or their content) that are not owned by the publisher.

Library of Congress Cataloging-in-Publication Data
Names: Hasekura, Isuna, 1982– author. | Bernhardt, Jasmine, translator. | Ayakura, Jyuu, 1981– artist.
Title: Wolf & Parchment : new theory Spice & Wolf / Isuna Hasekura ;
translation by Jasmine Bernhardt ; cover art by Jyuu Ayakura.
Other titles: Shinsetsu ookami to koshinryo: ookami to youhishi. English
Description: First Yen On edition. | New York, NY : Yen On, 2017–
Identifiers: LCCN 2017035577 | ISBN 9780316473453 (v. 1 : pbk.)
Subjects: CYAC: Adventure and adventurers—Fiction. | Fantasy. | BISAC: FICTION / Fantasy / Historical.
Classification: LCC PZ7.H2687 Wo 2017 | DDC [Fic]—dc23
LC record available at https://lccn.loc.gov/2017035577

ISBNs: 978-0-316-47345-3 (paperback)
978-0-316-47347-7 (ebook)

1 3 5 7 9 10 8 6 4 2

LSC-C

Printed in the United States of America

WOLF & PARCHMENT

WORLD MAP

DOLAN PLAINS

ROEF MOUNTAINS

ATIPH

YOITSU

NYOHHIRA

TAUSSIG

ROEF RIVER

KERUBE

SVERNEL

LESKO

TOLKIEN

KINGDOM OF WINFIEL

JIK

LENOS

ROAM RIVER

TEREO

PLOANIA

ENBERCH

KUMERSON

LAMTRA

N

TRENNI

W   E

POROSON

S

RUVINHEIGEN

ATIPH

YORENZ

SLAUDE RIVER

PASLOE

Map Illustration: Hidetada Idemitsu

PROLOGUE

The rain during the warm seasons was ever so slightly sweet. She thought this while licking away a raindrop that rolled down her cheek.

She had been given an errand, and on the way home, it started to rain. Like the region's never-ending plains, the rain, too, was flat. The raindrops, so small they were almost invisible, doused the peaceful fields, and white mist covered the land for as far as she could see. It was a quiet world—she only noticed the ground beneath her feet and the beating of her heart. If she stood still, it felt as though she would be trapped in place forever.

It was soft and calm, perfect for a nap—but if she had to be swallowed up, then somewhere else would be better. With this in mind, she quickened her pace.

Her skirt might have grown heavy with water and splattered with mud, but that did not concern her. She simply ran and ran.

Just as she began feeling as if she was caught in a bad dream, the wooden building appeared out of the mist.

The structure was quite old and slanted a bit, but she found the oddity of it appealing. When the two of them had first arrived, the shanty had been unfit for people to live inside, but they worked hard to repair it until she found herself rather attached. Were she to be stuck there for an eternity with no way out, she would not mind. In the end, that slanted roof would collapse on her like a hug, and she even thought that could be wonderful.

Picturing it, she smiled faintly.

Then, as though her footsteps echoed particularly loudly on this quiet, rainy day, the door to the shanty opened, and out came a person wearing white. Together they had repaired this place, driving in the last nail with their hands intertwined around the same hammer.

Seeing him, she lifted her head in happiness and widened her steps. A droplet fell into her mouth, and of course, it was sweet. As though pulled in by the taste, she jumped under the eaves.

It was not frightening if she closed her eyes. She knew he would catch her.

She leaped into his chest without waiting to catch her breath, declaring, "I'm home."

She could not hear an answer over her ragged breathing and the sound of her heart beating almost painfully in her chest.

But that did not matter. She knew he responded in kind.

It was only recently that she understood such thoughts were faith.

There was no one else in this misty rain.

Her eyes still closed, she repeated, "I'm home."

CHAPTER ONE

The day he set off was unusually sunny for winter. The blue sky seemed as though it might sweep him up, and the snow on the ground reflected the sunlight so brightly it hurt his eyes. Such beautiful, sunny winter days were rare in Nyohhira, a hot spring village deep in the northlands. It was a beautiful, picturesque day for departing on a journey, but it made him slightly nervous that this beginning might have consumed all his luck.

However, when he dropped his gaze to his long, rough traveling mantle, it reminded him of a traveling priest's garb. He reconsidered his fortune, thinking that there was no doubt this weather was a blessing from God for what was to come.

A pier jutted out into a river that flowed through the village. Though it was crowded during the changing of the seasons as guests came for the springs or returned home, only a single cargo boat was moored there now. The captain, a bearded, portly, middle-aged man, was currently carrying his passenger's luggage aboard while bustling about as though his vessel might sink at any moment. Contrary to his appearance, he moved to and fro easily and finished quickly.

"We'll be setting sail soon!"

The captain looked over and called out to him, and he waved instead of replying. Then, he took a deep breath and hauled his bag onto his shoulders. It was quite heavy, filled with gifts from those cheering him on.

"Col, do you have everything?"

Hearing his name, he turned around. Behind him stood the bathhouse master who had cared for him for over ten years and was now intently reviewing the luggage, Kraft Lawrence.

"You have money, a map, food, warm clothes, medicine, a short sword, and tinder, right?"

Lawrence, who was once widely known as a traveling merchant, busied himself with travel preparations. In fact, the one actually leaving on the journey was not nearly as conscientious as the more experienced man and relied on him completely.

"Sir, I'm sure he's checked at least that much. He doesn't have any more room, anyway."

The woman waiting beside Lawrence spoke with an exasperated chuckle. Her name was Hanna, and she ran the kitchen in Lawrence's bathhouse, Spice and Wolf.

"Oh, right. But still."

"It's all right, Mr. Lawrence. I once set off long ago with nothing but a single dried herring and whittled-down copper pieces."

When Col first met Lawrence, he was just a child of barely ten years. Back then, he visited the university cities in pursuit of knowledge as a wandering student, though that was merely in name. Truth be told, he was practically a beggar. With nowhere to go, he spent all his money and found himself lost in a foreign land with no one to depend on. Then, luck led him to Lawrence, the man who saved him.

That was already ten—no—fifteen years ago. Whenever he wondered if he had grown since then, doubt gnawed at him.

Lawrence's youthful looks had not changed very much, standing in front of him as he was, so Col was under the illusion that he was still a young boy.

But the hands pulling closed the string on his bag had grown sturdy from hard labor in the bathhouse. His current height dwarfed his diminutive stature as a child, and his once silvery hair now appeared almost gold.

Whether for good or ill, time flowed as it should.

"Well, yes, that's true...Plus, every clergyman acknowledges you as an intelligent young student now. I'm proud of you, too, and I could really stand to learn a thing or two from the late hours you keep for your studies."

"Please don't, sir. If you did that, I would have to spend even more time buying garlic and onions, so I'd rather you not."

Lawrence's compliment tickled him, but he shrank when Hanna spoke.

He always studied after his work for the day was done. What was more, he constantly struggled to keep his eyes open when he was working on manuscripts and reciting the scriptures. To stay awake, he would munch on raw onions and garlic, which resulted in countless lectures from Hanna because she wound up with no ingredients for cooking.

"But it's been more than ten years. Thank you for supporting the business until now. Our bathhouse only got this far because of you, Col. You were a big help," Lawrence said and spread his arms, pulling him into a big, strong, fatherly hug. Had he not met Lawrence, he did not know how he would have ended up. He should have been the one voicing his gratitude.

"No, thank you...I'm sorry for taking off during such a busy season."

"Oh no. We've kept you in the bathhouse for too long. But if you go south and make it big, at least let us know."

Lawrence, ever the quintessential merchant, always reassured Col like this.

"And…sorry the girls couldn't come see you off," he continued, his expression suddenly clouding.

"Holo already said her good-byes about a week ago. She said if she saw me off, she might try and stop me."

Holo was Lawrence's wife, and at times she acted like an elder sister or even second mother to young Col.

"She doesn't like to let people go. But maybe that's wise of her." Lawrence smiled dryly, and a sigh left his mouth.

"And I'm sorry Myuri has caused you so much trouble."

"Oh no…"

He was about to deny it, but he recalled the commotion of the past few days, especially the night before.

"Well…she was threatening me with her fangs and then she finally did bite me."

"Oh, boy."

Lawrence pressed his hand against his forehead, as though he was suffering from a headache. Myuri was Lawrence and Holo's only daughter, and she constantly wailed about wanting to leave the hot spring village and its remote region.

And when Col mentioned that he was about to set off on a journey, it was perfectly obvious what happened next.

"Both Myuri and Holo are strong of heart, but Holo knows when to give up and has the good judgment that comes with age. In that sense, Myuri is just like the midsummer sun."

Though she was his only daughter, more precious to him than anything in the world, Myuri's antics were the cause of Lawrence's aching temples. She had calmed down recently, but during her youth she had often gone out to play in the mountains and returned covered in blood.

Now, she had reached where talk of marriage was fast approaching, so that was something else to deal with.

"I haven't seen her all day. Maybe she's in the mountains, sulking and crying her eyes out to a bear," said Lawrence.

Col imagined Myuri clinging to the exasperated animal in its den, and he could not help but smile.

"When I've settled in, I'll send a letter. Please bring everyone for a visit when I do."

"Of course. But if you can, pick somewhere with lots of good food. Keeping those two happy during the trips is bound to be a hassle."

"I'll do that," Col responded with a smile as Lawrence extended his right hand. This was not the same person who had hired him, nor was it the one who had saved his life as a child ten years ago.

This was the master of a bathhouse, offering a handshake while seeing off a traveler.

"Take care." As if he had noticed Col's inadvertent tears, Lawrence smiled even bigger and gripped his hand harder.

"Be careful of unboiled water and raw food."

"You too, Ms. Hanna...Be well."

He tried his hardest to hide the effect of his stuffed nose on his voice as he shook her hand as well. Then he hoisted up his bag.

"Hey, are you ready?!" the boat captain called. He must have been paying careful attention, because he chose the perfect moment.

"I'm coming!" Col called back, looking at Lawrence and Hanna. Once he left, it was possible he would not see them for many years or ever again. It might also be the last time he ever laid eyes on Nyohhira and the rising steam from its hot baths.

His legs would not move no matter how hard he tried, and that was when Lawrence patted him on the shoulder.

"Go, lad. Venture out into a new world!"

It would be false of him not to respond.

"Don't call me lad. I'm already the age you were when I first met you!"

He took the first step, the second shortly followed, and he did not even think of the third.

When he looked back, Lawrence was smiling calmly with his hands clasped behind his back, and Hanna was waving modestly. He shifted his gaze beyond them, more reluctant than ever to part with the village of Nyohhira, and he wondered if that tomboy Myuri was there. He would have liked to see her pouting face peeking out from behind a tree, but there was no sight of the young girl. She was just as stubborn as her mother. He smiled a little and walked toward the pier.

"Did you finish saying your good-byes?"

"Sorry to keep you waiting."

"That's the life of a captain for you. You can't go down the same river twice. Not that regrets are a bad thing, though."

Steering a boat along the quiet rivers every day must naturally bring one wisdom.

Col nodded deeply at the captain's words and boarded the vessel from the pier.

"You're my only passenger. Feel free to take a nap on that pile of furs," the captain said as he undid the rope tying down the boat.

At the phrase "pile of furs," a memory surfaced in the young man's mind, a story he had heard long ago.

A young traveling peddler had stopped in a certain village, and as was his custom, he spent the night in his wagon curled up atop his cargo of furs. When he did, a beautiful young girl appeared, asking him to bring her to her hometown. She had flaxen hair that was especially beautiful under the moonlight, as well as animal ears atop her head and a tail with the most exquisite fur on her behind. She called herself the wisewolf—the incarnation of a wolf that lived in the village's wheat and commanded the harvest, a being who had lived for hundreds of years and would for many more. The peddler accepted the girl's request, and together they set out on a journey. Together they experienced joy and sorrow, shared their feelings for each other, and then lived happily ever after. The end.

Unable to imagine such a thing happening to him, he entered the pile of furs and groped around. It was all right. No one was hiding in them.

Along with his impromptu bedding, the boat was crammed with barrels and sacks full of charcoal. The barrels were likely filled with leftover tree resin from the charcoal production process. The waterproof substance could be applied to prevent molding, and its strong burnt smell wafted toward him occasionally. The furs came from communities sprinkled through the mountains beyond Nyohhira. The people who inhabited these areas worked hard at hunting during the winter, and the sales from the pelts allowed them to purchase things they needed in town. It would be too much trouble for them to carry their wares all the way to market, so the furs were usually gathered in Nyohhira before being shipped off by boat. The same went for the charcoal and resin.

"There's a lot of furs this year."

"Yeah, business has been booming, fortunately. Nyohhira has always been very prosperous, but things are picking up everywhere now. You know the war between the northern lands and the southern Church ended years back, right? That reckless fight was over long ago, but the official end of the hostilities has made a tremendous difference," the captain explained earnestly, heaving up the rope before hopping on board himself.

Strangely, the boat did not rock at all.

"Once we set off, it's the beginning of your journey."

Facing astern, the captain took hold of the pole. The craft slid forward slowly, gliding along the river's surface. Though it was an ordinary day in Nyohhira's long winter, the familiar sights of the village seemed different from the boat. This may very well be the first or even last time he saw Nyohhira as a traveler. When this thought crossed his mind, he suddenly could not help sitting up on his knees. Then, he waved to Lawrence and Hanna as they watched from the riverside.

"Thank you!"

Lawrence smiled and raised his hand casually. Hanna wore the same expression she did when the results of her cooking were satisfactory.

And before he knew it, they, too, vanished from sight. Mountain rivers flowed quickly.

"Well, you've said your good-byes. Now it's time to look ahead," the captain said to the young man staring back toward the village. His tone was not commanding but gentle, as if to encourage the young man. Slightly self-conscious, he gave the captain a strained smile and faced forward.

Ah, I'm leaving on a journey—a strangely sad yet exciting feeling wrapped around him.

"You were searching around in those furs a moment ago, weren't you? Was there a rat or something?"

"Huh? Ah…Actually, I was remembering a story."

Thus he told the captain about the meeting of the peddler and the wolf spirit. Such fantastic stories were everywhere, but the captain seemed quite interested.

"There will be plenty of opportunity to tell those kinds of stories to while away the time on our voyage. It's great if there's more. But searching around in the fur after remembering that story means you're pretty superstitious for a young one."

The captain would never believe him if Col said it was a true story, and if he mentioned that the daughter of that wolf could be hiding in the furs, the news might shock him. After all, the peddler in the tale was Lawrence, and the wolf hiding in his cargo was Holo.

Col had joined them on their extraordinary journey and assisted them in grand, dizzying adventures. Just recalling those memories stirred his excitement, though plenty of his experiences were terrifying as well.

But the biggest surprise after being swept up in their story did not come from the heart-pounding, blood-pumping moments. It was what he saw accompanying them in their life after their happily ever after.

He was astonished at their continued life of happiness, and he could do nothing but laugh.

"So how far are you going to go? You said Svernel for now, right?" The captain named a town that lay to the west down the river, then south by land—a town that had long prospered from trade of furs and amber.

"I will first gather information about my journey there. After that, I plan to head to Lenos."

"Oh, Lenos! I know that town. It's on a big river with ships always coming and going! I've heard that means plenty of checkpoints, too."

Col knew it well. He had met Lawrence and Holo at one of those very checkpoints along the waterway.

"I see. What are you going to do there? Craftwork? Doesn't seem likely...Trade, then?"

"No." He shook his head a little and looked up at the sky, swearing an oath to the presence that should be there. "I want to become a clergyman."

"Well, I didn't know you were a priest! My, my."

"But I'm still in training, so I don't know if I can become one."

"Ha-ha-ha. Don't say that—it sounds like you don't believe in God's protection."

That was true.

"But see, isn't the Church involved in a big brouhaha with the Kingdom of Winfiel right now?"

The captain lowered the pole deep into the river, and the front of the boat turned to avoid a large rock. The mountains around Nyohhira contained no open fields with natural vistas. Snow piled high on the sheer cliffs, and even farther up, deer stared down at them in wonder.

"You know quite a lot."

"Rivers carry not just water, but information as well."

Apparently, the captain's show of knowledge was deliberate. He was a cheerful person.

The river met the ocean west of here, and the Kingdom of Winfiel was a large island nation to the southwest of that. It was famous for wool and, lately, a flourishing ship manufacturing industry.

It had been a few years since the beginning of the dispute between the kingdom and the pope who led the Church overseeing the world's faith.

"And they say the commotion started all because of taxes, right? That's directly relevant to people who work in transport, like me. You hear about it even if you don't want to."

When a boat sailed downriver, it would pass through the lands of many lords. Every checkpoint the captain had to pass meant a tax, and there could be fifty or more along a big river. In some places, there were over a hundred.

In addition, though lords only charged tolls for their own territory, the Church could levy taxes in every place its teachings spread, which effectively meant the entire world. These collections were called "tithes."

"If we could avoid paying tithes, it would be a big help for us. What's more, those funds were originally gathered for the fight against pagans. There's no reason to collect it anymore since that war is over. We owe it to the king of Winfiel for speaking up."

Taxes for any reason were always unpopular. There was no reason to speak ill of a king who wished to get rid of one.

"And look at how the pope treats a ruler who makes sense! Boy, I'm really rooting for the king of Winfiel...," the captain said before suddenly closing his mouth. He seemed to remember that his passenger wished to work as a holy man. "Sorry about that. I don't mean to speak badly about your aspirations."

"No," Col said shortly with a little smile. "I agree with you."

"Oh?"

He narrowed his eyes—not because of the captain's puzzled stare, but because of the cool, clear wind that blew from downstream.

"I can't believe that, in order to force the payment of taxes, the pope ordered the kingdom to suspend all religious practices without consultation."

His white breath grew even whiter, likely from his anger. This suspension was an order from the pope, which meant all those who served the Church in that area were without work.

"For three years now, there have been no baptisms, no weddings between people who love each other, and no funerals for the cherished deceased in the kingdom. They are all important ceremonies in life that the clergy administer, and the pope has obstructed them all. I cannot see how forcing us to pay taxes to earn God's good grace is in accordance to the Lord's will. I am uneducated and powerless, but..."

He gripped the wooden crest of the Church that always hung around his neck and lay against his chest.

"I wish to help in correcting these corrupted teachings of God."

In order to save the Kingdom of Winfiel from the arrogant pope, who neglected the salvation of souls for three years all because of money—and so he could rectify the divine teachings—Col would have to fight. That was why he left on his journey.

There would be hardships. There would be suffering. But he had learned much thus far, and he had even come to meet Lawrence and his wife Holo, the miraculous pair from a fairy tale. He could do it. There was no doubt.

He wanted to bestow at least a few smiles and some happiness upon this irrational, cruel world.

He stared beyond the river and vowed to himself once again.

God, give me strength and guidance.

He closed his eyes and felt a strong wind, as though an angel was stroking his cheek.

"Haaaah…"

When he heard the captain sigh behind him, he abruptly came back to earth.

Col's face flushed—he was barely even a priest's apprentice.

"Er, well, that is what I wish anyhow…"

"Oh, well, I was certain that it was because you were jealous of all the clergymen eating and drinking at the hot springs while you were working in Nyohhira."

The captain spoke bluntly, but there was truth behind his assumption, too. In order to visit such a remote mountain place, one needed enough funds to travel and a job that could be abandoned for months at a time without trouble. Those with both were mostly retired heads of large companies, nobles whose governance was going smoothly, and high-ranking clergymen.

"Of course, many wish to work in the Church for that reason. It is reprehensible, though…"

"It's not unusual for a priest to have lots of 'nieces' and 'nephews.'"

Though the captain appeared to be implying something, it was not as if the underlying meaning was his own opinion. It was more like an open secret. Priests were required to stay celibate, so of course, they could not have children without wives. Therefore, they had so-called nieces and nephews instead. Not even the pope was an exception to this—one of his "nieces" had been married off to the Kingdom of Winfiel, so these corrupt practices were growing commonplace.

"I constantly wish for the world to be a more honest, straightforward place. It isn't, so even the pope throws his weight around for the sake of money," Col said with a sigh, and the captain responded as though searching for the right words.

"So what? You mean you've never laid a single finger on a dancing girl in Nyohhira?" he asked, as though such a thing was impossible. Col merely responded with pride.

"Of course I haven't."

"Well, that's…"

The captain was at a loss.

Col was used to this kind of response. There were very few real priests who upheld their vows of abstinence. The ones who did as they should were monks who lived in remote monasteries, where it was a struggle to even make contact with a woman.

"Even if I wanted to break the vows of asceticism, I don't think I could," Col said with a wry smile, and the captain finally smiled, too, though uncomfortably.

Dancers and daughters of musicians did call out to him sometimes, though they were only teasing. And because of that, he most likely could not say that he had ever needed to expend much effort upholding his vows.

"However, I think we should maintain what has been established."

Col straightened his posture as he spoke.

"Hmm. Yeah," the captain murmured keenly and again changed the direction of the ship's bow. "That being said, the world is like a river. You can never go as straight as you like." He turned around, and the expression on the captain's face was not smug, nor did it sneer at the ideals of a young man.

It was that of a hermit who had weathered a great many things and tried to play them off calmly.

"But those periodic twists and turns give fish a place to live."

He must have spent plenty of time lost in thought while working as a ship captain, because his words were actually quite profound. In fact, a famous theologist had reached a similar truth after being surrounded by destruction.

"I think I understand what you mean."

"Of course, I don't mean to criticize anyone's ideals. Especially not one who wants to be a priest. But if you stick to one path the whole time, there's lots of things you'll never know. You gain experience because you make detours."

Col honestly agreed.

Still, he could not see where the captain's explanation was headed.

"Um…in summary?"

For some reason, the man rubbed his nose awkwardly.

"Mm. Well, you know. I see that the purpose and spirit of your journey are remarkable, but…Well, I didn't think you'd be so strict about it, so maybe I've just been a useless busybody…"

"Huh?"

It happened right after he asked.

"Well, there's no turning back at this point. You can come out now," the captain said to the cargo. He was not looking at the pile of furs, but rather the barrels in front of them. And then, *bam!* The lid of one barrel flew off.

"Whoops." The captain skillfully caught the lid.

Sticking out from the barrel was a pair of skinny legs shod with rough traveling shoes. Ignoring the captain's troubled smile, Col could not close his gaping mouth.

"Ooh! Oooooooh!"

There came a groan, and a hand gripped the brim as the barrel shuddered.

Just as it was about to topple over, a single girl popped out from inside.

"Pee-yoooooou!"

"Myuri?!"

The girl springing from the barrel scattered the mountain of furs with a kick and jumped into Col's chest. She had strangely colored hair, like flecks of silver mixed into ash, and a slender frame. At a little older than ten years, she was still too juvenile to be called a young lady. She was full of enough energy to bowl him over, and the boat rocked back and forth. The only reason it did not tip over was most likely thanks to the captain's skill.

"Ah, M-Myuri, wh-why—?"

The words, *You're here,* and then, *You smell burned,* were caught in his throat and did not come out.

"Why nothing!"

The girl, Myuri, yelled with all her might, and with tears welling in her eyes, perhaps because of the awful smell in the barrel, she looked down at him.

"Take me with you!"

Tears more heated than the hot springs rolled down her cheeks. But with Myuri's sudden emergence from the barrel, the undeniable implication that she and the captain had worked together, and that now the boat could not turn back—all these things had

to be addressed later. The emotions of the girl in front of him seemed liable to explode at any moment, and her ashen hair was already wiggling.

He had no other choice. He hurriedly pulled her into a hug and hid her small head in his arms.

"All right! I said all right!"

Calm down!

Then, she broke loose from his arms, and her face snapped up toward his.

"Really?! Really?!"

"Yes, really, so please calm down—"

Your ears and tail are sticking out!

Ignoring all the screaming in his heart, Myuri opened her eyes wide and grinned with satisfaction, pulling him into a hug like a wolf devouring its prey.

"I love you, Brother! Thank you!"

The beast's tail that was the same color as her hair swished back and forth quite enthusiastically, betraying her tremendous delight.

His face blanched, and he eyed the captain, who was sitting at the stern of the boat and opening a small wine cask, thankfully not paying attention to them. He must have been relieved that the secret was out or had oddly taken a hint.

In any case, he had to do something about the situation now. The story of the peddler and the wolf was a true story, and this girl was their only daughter. Normally, she could show and hide her ears and tail at will and dressed like a typical person, but when she was excited or surprised, her hidden ears and tail had the troubling quirk of revealing themselves regardless of her intentions.

"Myuri, Myuri…!"

"Heh-heh, eh-heh-heh…Hmm?"

She could smile so happily even when her tears were not yet dry.

It was a good thing to be so rich in emotion.

But he still wanted her to be a bit more thoughtful.

"They're out, they're coming out…!"

After hearing Col's whispers, Myuri finally noticed. Like a cat washing its face, she hurriedly and vigorously rubbed her head. Once her tail had also vanished, it appeared they had managed to avoid revealing anything to the captain. Relieved, Col relaxed his neck, and the back of his head fell with a *thud* onto the bottom of the boat.

And then he sat straight up again.

"Myuri."

"Hmm?"

The expression she showed him was clearly forced. It was a woman's smile that she had started making whenever his voice filled with anger.

"Move."

"…Okay."

More reasonable than usual, her pleasant mask disappeared, as though she thought she could not hide on such a small boat or as though she had made a promise.

"Honestly…," he said, sighing, as he was about to pull himself up, when Myuri held out her hand.

Together they put away the scattered furs and returned the barrel Myuri was hiding in to its previous spot.

It was originally a barrel for tree resin, so it reeked of something burnt. Myuri smelled like she had been dropped into the ashes of a hearth. The wolf's blood that flowed in her veins gave her an exceptional sense of smell; if she had endured such misery, then she must have been determined.

What was more, this girl was the daughter of Lawrence and

Holo. She would not run sobbing to a bear's den if she was not taken along on a journey.

"And?" Col asked after everything had been put back into place.

"Eh-heh-heh...I ran away from home."

Myuri shrugged as she spoke, playing meek when she actually was not, ever a tomboy.

They could not turn the boat back at this point. The river flowing out from the rugged mountains was surrounded on both sides by tall cliffs and, at best, rocky stretches. Of course, even if they were able to berth there, it was unlikely that there would be proper roads. Though travelers could follow the mountain paths from the checkpoints that the lords built, some would lead away from Nyohhira. Furthermore, winter still tightly gripped the region, leaving snow piled high and the weather ready to take a turn for the worse in an instant. A lone girl could never endure those conditions with such skinny legs. It was clear they could not send her back right away, so Col sat facing Myuri and sighing deeply.

"What are you wearing?"

As Myuri sat properly and patiently, her expression suddenly brightened.

"Isn't it cute? Miss Helen made them for me. She said that everyone in the south dresses like this."

The name Myuri mentioned belonged to a popular dancer and customer at the bathhouse. The girl before him was wearing a rabbit fur cape on her shoulders, a decorated shirt with puffy shoulders, and a corset of bearskin (or something of the like). If his knowledge was correct, the outfit was similar to what the court nobles wore several decades ago.

But the greatest cause of his headache was further down.

"It's too bad I'm not as thick as Miss Helen...Eh-heh-heh, still, what do you think?"

Her slim legs were wrapped in two close-fitting tubes of linen that had been stitched together. The short trousers she wore over them were cut to a daring height—they were meant to show off everything below them. She was even sporting her rough traveling shoes, not for any practical purpose, but likely to emphasize her slender limbs.

"Well, I'm not sure where to begin, but it is not proper for a young girl to show so much of her legs."

"I'm not showing anything. These cover everything to my toenails!" Myuri insisted, tugging on the embroidered fabric covering her thin legs. Her gestures were oddly suggestive, and Col involuntarily cleared his throat.

"I am not talking about covering your skin."

Her appearance was a far cry from that of the plain village girls with their hair in braids and their linen skirts and aprons.

"First, these are not travel appropriate. You're freezing, aren't you?"

"I'm okay. Miss Helen and the others said that beauty is pain!" Myuri claimed with a big grin, but upon closer observation, Col could see that her lips were pale and her legs were shivering like a baby deer's.

He heaved a deep sigh, reaching out to the stack of furs, and began piling them on her lap.

"I was so relieved when you finally stopped digging up hibernating frogs and throwing them into the baths and setting traps for rabbits and squirrels, but..."

Myuri used to be so energetic she drew attention even when she was together with the village boys. Then one day, she suddenly became more feminine, which relieved Col a little. Now she was making him worry in all-new ways.

Since making guests happy was a key part of working at a bathhouse, their business was a showy and animated place. The visiting patrons were all the type to make merry, so preaching to Myuri about abstinence and asceticism was not effective.

Myuri's father, Lawrence, would scold her once, and if her behavior improved even a little, he would not say anything more. Myuri had discovered this, so reprimands were no longer a reliable deterrent. And finally, she had recently learned to mournfully say, *"But I thought it would make you happy, Father...,"* and so it was no use.

Her mother, Holo, knew that Lawrence's scoldings were no match for the fear of having one's tail stepped on, so Myuri usually tried to gauge her expression. However, Holo, who would yet live for hundreds of years, was not the kind to mind one or two pieces of fabric and was rather more likely to gather information about flamboyant clothes from Myuri.

In the end, Col was the only one who could be strict with her.

"But you were the one who told me to dress more like a girl, Brother."

In the pile of furs, Myuri huffed.

"You're taking it too far. I said that because you would go into the mountains dressed like a savage, with a single loincloth on. It is important to do everything in moderation. Do you understand?"

"...Yeah," Myuri replied flatly, collapsing into the pile of furs, facing away from him. "Eh-heh-heh, but it's fine. I'm finally out of that little village," she said and stretched out her arms, looking up at the clear blue sky.

He did not want to constantly dampen her enthusiasm, but someone had to play that role.

"When we reach Svernel, we'll find you some people and a horse to take you back."

If they went to that town, they would find many friendly acquaintances among those who supplied Nyohhira's bath-houses. They were all trustworthy folk, so he could safely entrust Myuri to them.

Still, though his stomach tensed for Myuri's inevitable fit, it did not seem she would raise a fuss about the plan.

"Myuri?"

Col called out to her again, and still staring up at the sky, Myuri slowly closed her eyes and sighed.

"Fine."

She was being very reasonable, and that gave him a sinking feeling instead. Or perhaps she simply wanted to leave the village for a bit? But would that warrant the determination to hold her breath in a barrel that would burn her nostrils with its awful stench? What was more, she had spent the week leading up to the day of his departure literally nipping at him.

Suspiciously, Col studied her carefully, but Myuri simply yawned.

"*Faaahh...Hah.* I started getting ready before dawn, so I'm tired..."

No matter how much he worried, none of it reached her. To the carefree Myuri, everything was a nuisance. Her boldness was abnormal, and that was clear from her talent—she could fall asleep no matter what the situation once she decided she wanted to sleep. He could already hear her snoring softly from the pile of furs.

Col sighed in relief, piled some more pelts on Myuri, and removed the ones on top of her head that seemed to be causing her distress. Her expression when she slept was pure and adorable, but that very cuteness always gave him something to worry about.

Once he finished covering her in furs to make sure she was

28

sleeping warmly, the captain skillfully hooked the handle of a wooden mug with the pole and extended it to Col. He could tell it was currant liquor from the tangy scent.

"She came to me while I was catching some shut-eye in the town meeting hall before dawn."

Col immediately knew he was talking about Myuri. Of course, he had no intentions of reproaching the captain for helping her with her plans.

"She cried, 'Let me on your boat—I'll die if you don't!' I didn't know if it was a trick of the moonlight or something, but when I saw those golden eyes shining in the darkness, I thought, *she's serious.*"

Sipping the liquor, more sour than sweet, Col's smile twitched. He had experienced all this past week how forceful Myuri was when she asked to be taken on the journey.

"Well, you come across aimless wanderers and people who have good reasons to run away every so often in this work. You should have good enough judgment to know if you should help or not."

"And that was enough for you?"

"Well, her traveling companion was a straitlaced young man. But he was more serious than I imagined, and I was nervous that he might get angry."

The captain was smiling, but he spoke with a sigh. He took a sip of the piquant liquor and slumped his shoulders.

At any rate, once they reached Svernel, he would send Myuri back. He did not know what she was planning, but he had to be resolute about this. Myuri was carefree, self-willed, and the kind of girl who would perform in distracting outfits with the other dancers if the patrons encouraged her to, but she was usually calm. As she grew up, she began developing a shocking resemblance to her mother, though the true similarity lay not in her looks but in her intellectual eyes. Those eyes that bore straight through fate, that appeared between her bouts of horseplay, were the same as those of her mother, who was once revered as the wisewolf.

"But I didn't expect you'd be siblings. I was sure you were romantically involved, but I was off on that mark."

"We're not siblings by blood. She's the only daughter of the bathhouse master who took care of me. I heard her cry when she was born, and I always had to change her diapers."

Even Myuri herself had thought he was really her older brother until recently. It truly showed how Holo and Lawrence treated him not as a mere helper but as family. He could not thank them enough.

"Well, with such a lively girl, I'm sure your long journey will be brighter."

Col planned to send Myuri back to the village as soon as he could, but he could easily imagine that the trip would not be quiet or simple until then.

"I don't mind her energy, but I want her to act appropriately."

"That's important, too. Like the flow of the river."

The captain smiled and raised his mug lightly, so Col, too, raised his in response and prayed to God for the safety of their travels.

The boat passed through several checkpoints, and each time they stopped, they had their cargo inspected and paid tax.

Myuri awoke after noon and watched everything around her with great interest as though it was new, so she was unusually quiet.

As the sun grew red in the sky, the scenery around them also changed. Though mountains still surrounded them, there was less snow and more riverbanks filled with pebbles, and they could occasionally spot roads running along the river.

The river, whose current had also grown much gentler, made a wide detour around a hill, and on the other side was a checkpoint bigger and livelier than any they had seen before.

"Whoa! This is incredible!" Myuri exclaimed.

Piles of cargo were lined up on the riverbank. The goods must have been transported via the river, or perhaps they would be carried to the next checkpoint even farther down. On the entrance to the pier stood armored soldiers carrying spears and preparing torches for the night watch. Other people were tying the boats to the pier, announcing that there were no more ships going out today, and still others were already on their boats, drinking merrily.

"This is Lord Havlish's checkpoint, the second biggest on this river."

As the captain brought the boat into the pier, some of the other pilots who seemed to be familiar with him offered their greetings.

"The second biggest? This is the second biggest?"

Beyond the riverbed, they could see two inns with chairs and tables placed outside under the eaves, and festivities for the evening were already starting. There were no stifling city walls, so the scene seemed quite calm.

"The biggest one is another two nights down the river. It doesn't have these little inns nearby. There's a magnificent stone fortress with a bell tower and a gigantic chain that connects it to another stone tower on the opposite shore. When you pass under that chain over your head, you get all nervous because it feels like you're being judged in hell."

"A chain?" Myuri seemed puzzled. "But boats can't pass through if there's a chain there, right?"

Her confusion apparently amused the captain, and she turned to Col for help.

"That's the point," he said.

"Right. The sea is right there. They drop the chain when they need to for protection, so that the pirates from the open seas don't come inland. It also might be a warning to pirates—that if they attack the towns, they'll be tied up in those chains and sentenced to work like slaves."

As though the chain were directly above her now, Myuri opened her eyes wide.

"Pi...rates...? Pirates?! You mean, those kinds of pirates?!"

For Myuri, who had been born and raised in Nyohhira, where even the highest mountain points only granted views of more jagged peaks, it was an unfamiliar word.

She opened her eyes even wider in excitement and gripped Col's arm enough to hurt him.

"Wow! Pirates, Brother! Pirates?! With that? The chain?!"

The captains around them glanced curiously in their direction as Myuri danced in excitement. But when they somehow understood that this girl had just come down from the mountains, they smiled gently like grandparents fawning over their grandchildren and almost seemed about to transform into pirates themselves at any moment.

"Wow, cool! Brother, are you going out to sea, too? You are, right?"

"No," Col said even more coolly than usual. If Myuri grew any more excited, her ears and tail might appear.

And more importantly, if she became too interested in the outside world, it would be difficult to send her back to Nyohhira.

"Pirates almost never come inland, and I've never heard of it happening."

"Well, sure. It's just a threat...or maybe just a display, saying that this place is important enough to be targeted by pirates. Anyone, whether they came down the river or from out at sea, anyone would be petrified to see those huge chains above them."

Myuri nodded vigorously at every word and sighed in admiration.

"The outside world is complicated," she said, seriously enough that a cry of *Oh, God!* could have followed. Col could not help but smile.

But he could not let his guard down. He had to maintain as much distance as possible and keep a level head.

"Let's go, Myuri. We will be staying here tonight."

"Oh, uh, okay!"

Staring docilely down the river, Myuri returned to her senses and hurriedly retrieved her things from the barrel she had hidden in. He did not know what she might have packed, but it seemed that she did make some preparations for traveling.

"Thank you for taking us on your boat."

"Don't mention it."

Myuri realized that this would be good-bye for the vessel's captain, and she waved with a smile, readjusting her shoulder bag that was the same as Col's.

"Thank you, captain!"

"Bye now!"

In response to her carefree smile, the captain waved the pole he used to steer the boat. Smiling, Myuri nodded, and as they left, she turned back to him again and waved.

Col watched her out of the corner of his eye as they walked along the pier, their feet raising a *clop, clop* sound on the wood. Once they stepped down onto the road formed by the rocks of the riverbank, he felt relieved to be back on firm ground. Traveling by boat was convenient, but it made him slightly uneasy. He glanced at Myuri to check if she had gotten seasick, and her expression was clouded.

"Are you feeling nauseous?"

Myuri looked up and smiled weakly.

"No. We'd just made friends with him…I'm a bit sad."

She forced a smile, which made her look quite pitiful when coupled with her small, thin frame and cold dress.

But he could not let that show in his expression. He collected himself and spoke.

"You part with many people at the bathhouse."

"Yeah, but…guests are guests."

"From his point of view, you're just another guest, Myuri."

"…"

Walking beside him, she looked up, her expression slightly hurt.

"Oh…"

Traveling was a series of meetings and partings. Not every part of it was fun.

If Myuri understood this, then there was a chance she might go back to Nyohhira without a fight.

But even as Col thought all this, he could not help his heartache when he saw how deflated she was.

"Well, he'll keep sailing up and down this river. If he returns to the village port, then you can see him anytime."

Myuri lifted her gaze to him. When their eyes met, she smiled in relief.

"Thanks, Brother."

Her smile almost moved him.

Together, they headed to the inn on the riverbank and secured a room. He had originally planned on staying in the cheapest shared room available, but since Myuri was with him, he had no choice. To make up for it, he would simply need to be more frugal down the road.

He set his things down in relief, while Myuri opened the

wooden window and looked down outside. She turned back to him in excitement.

"Brother! They're cooking meat outside!"

Having been raised in Nyohhira, Myuri loved dinner parties enough as it was. She loved good food even more, and once she came of age, she would surely be unable to resist liquor.

She pulled him by the sleeve to look out the window, and sure enough, some people were in the middle of roasting a luxurious whole pig in a hearth surrounded by stone.

"See? See? They're roasting a pig. That's so cool. I wonder if there's a festival or something."

Nyohhira could hold its own as a bustling locale, but the variety of goods in the hot spring village was limited due to its location deep in the mountains. The inhabitants could hunt deer and rabbits in their area, but since they could not obtain pigs, the roast seemed like a luxury import to them. It was an even rarer sight to see a pig being cooked whole.

Ignoring Myuri as she was consumed with excitement, Col thought about how he could convince her to make do with tonight's dinner of dried meats and poached beans when he felt someone's gaze on him. Among the travelers and craftsmen drinking together below, a single person sat alone, looking up and waving at him.

"Hey, Brother, just a bit, please?" Myuri pestered him, and he took several copper coins from his wallet and placed them firmly in her hand.

"Buy food for both of us. It won't be much, but you should be able to get some of the roasted pig."

"Oh…Okay."

Myuri seemed perplexed by the copper *dip* coins in her hand, which were commonly used in this region.

"Brother, what about you? You're not coming?"

"I have my daily prayer and recitation of the scripture. Or would you rather join me here?"

An expression of displeasure abruptly appeared, and she made her way to the door, leaving a wide margin between them so as not to get dragged in.

"I'll be right back!"

"No alcohol."

"Aww…"

"I said no."

Myuri did not respond and left the room, still pouting.

Col sighed in exasperation. He checked the view outside after a while, and Myuri, jogging up to the roast pig, suddenly turned back in his direction and waved. She immediately stood out in a crowd, though not because she wore the unusual clothes that the dancers had told her about. She herself was striking. Almost as though she had been cut out around the edges and surrounded by a faint glow.

Perhaps he was also seeing her in a favorable light because he had always fawned over her like a real little sister.

As he smiled dryly, a knock sounded at the door.

"Come in."

Col's happy expression faded, and he closed the window.

Then, he opened the door, and standing outside was the traveler who had looked up at him from the square just a little while ago.

While the traveler was rather small in stature, that was not to say he was very short. He was not particularly sturdy, but he was far from skinny. Perhaps his enigmatic impression was because he worked as something similar to a spy.

He looked like a young man when wearing a hood, but in

actuality, he was a very quiet adult with the beginnings of wrinkles appearing on his face.

"I'm surprised. I did not expect to see you here."

Col offered him a seat, but the man shook his head.

"I will not stay long. Sorry to make you clear the area."

"Ah…That girl forced me to take her along from Nyohhira. She hid herself in the cargo. It was a barrel filled with resin, and I thought, surely she wouldn't be in such a putrid place."

"Oh?" The man was surprised, and his shoulders shook with laughter. "Those barrels are indeed smelly. I've hid in them many a time."

It did seem that such rough work was not uncommon. This man was a messenger for a large and powerful organization known as the Debau Company, a group that held sway over the entirety of the northlands. The Debau Company sided with the Winfiel Kingdom, which was currently in conflict with the pope. The group was most likely aiming to extract some special trading privileges by pulling the kingdom out of hot water.

Therefore, it acted as a line of communication between the kingdom and those who wished to support it, like Col.

"I don't find it humorous…but why are you here? I thought we were to meet in Svernel?"

"About that—no more trips to Lenos. I was waiting here to tell you. Instead, I need you to head to Atiph."

"Atiph?"

That was the name of the settlement by the checkpoint with the large chain to ward off pirates. The captain had told them about it on the boat earlier that day.

"That's quite far from Lenos…Did something happen?"

The river flowed south from Nyohhira for a bit before changing its course due west. After meandering through the narrow mountain ranges, it entered flatlands called the Dolan Plains and eventually emptied into the sea. Lenos was a town that was farther southwest, beyond several mountains.

"The negotiations with the archbishop at the cathedra there collapsed almost immediately."

"What...?"

"Heir Hyland wanted to attend to it in person, but since it is an important area that connects the north and the south, Duke Laforque will oversee the negotiations instead."

When Col was a child, the town of Lenos did not even have a church yet, but these days the scale of worship there had reached the point where it could be called the great center of faith in the northlands. It had been close to ten years since the establishment of the cathedrae, which had the authority to command priests in other churches, and almost ten years since the archbishop first held the priest's staff.

Col's spirits fell, though it was not because negotiations at the important town of Lenos had not gone well.

"Much to Heir Hyland's chagrin, I'm sure."

He was worried about that particular person.

"Why fret? The good thing about him is that he doesn't give up."

Hyland had a high status and the blood of Winfiel royalty, but the messenger spoke of him as though he was a friend. Typically, this would be disrespectful, but Col understood how the man felt. Hyland had an oddly unassuming, straightforward nature, which made it easy to think of him as a close acquaintance.

Of course, Col had decided to help the Kingdom of Winfiel because it was a reasonable thing to do, but it was also because Hyland had come to soak in the waters of Nyohhira and asked for his help directly.

"Then, will the next negotiations be in Atiph? But using Atiph after Lenos..."

"You mean since the negotiations in Lenos have failed, they're already obsolete?"

Prompted by the man, Col nodded compliantly.

"Even with a cathedra at the church in Atiph, a newcomer is still a newcomer. It's a lesser one for sure. But these past few years, the entire town has really benefited from trade, and it appears they will continue to grow. If we can convince them, we could secure a third of the northern sea."

If the Debau Company, the ruler of every corner of the northlands, said such a thing, then it was certain.

Additionally, Col was unaware of the news that Atiph had grown so quickly. One always ended up out of the loop in the remote mountains of Nyohhira.

"Moreover, Atiph is an autonomous city not subject to any particular royal authority, so it isn't a bad place to begin. If they respond favorably to our persuasion, then other free city-states may follow suit. More importantly, it takes less than two days to reach the Winfiel Kingdom from Atiph on the sea routes nowadays. It seems far on a map, but it is actually a crucial town."

Col did have some confidence in his knowledge of geography, but the world was shifting a great deal. Perhaps it would be best to think of what he remembered as a thing of the past.

"In any case, we need Heir Hyland and the Kingdom of Winfiel to work as hard as they can. There's no profit for us in following blindly."

He smiled wryly at the man's merchantlike choice of words, but it was the truth.

"Sir Col, you have a goal in mind as well, no? Aiming for the seat of the royal family's priest?"

"Well…"

He was about to argue, but he faltered. Instead, he smiled shyly, admitting his own desires.

"I cannot say that I am uninterested in being successful. However, I cannot accept the pope's frankly tyrannical policies and this status quo in which God's teachings are being used so arbitrarily. Most of all, I was touched to see Heir Hyland so firm in his faith. I would very much like for someone like him to rule. If I could be of assistance to proper worship, then I would be most pleased. And..."

"And?"

"If the tithes grow stronger, then the price of goods coming into Nyohhira will go up, right? So if we instead eliminate them, then we can protect Nyohhira's profits."

The other man seemed rather surprised and smacked his forehead, smiling.

"You're different from the monks holed up studying in monasteries, Sir Col. You are truly reassuring. You firmly grasp the scales in your right hand and the scriptures in your left."

"Or perhaps I don't have a good hold of either."

"That's something you show little by little as you go."

And thus everyone would gain what they wished for in the end. Though Col himself was one of the potential beneficiaries, it was not as if he had no interest in simply wanting to work with Hyland. It would be an exaggeration, however, to say he would do it without any compensation.

He could still clearly remember his talk with Hyland, soaking in the silent grotto bath that was only for the use of distinguished guests, wishing to go through the catechisms. Hyland's faith and passion were real, and his heart truly ached for his country as it faced hardships brought on by the pope's whims. From time immemorial, the clergymen who stood beside those in power were also often their friends. Col could stand proud if everything he had learned up until that point in life could be used to support such a wonderful person.

"And I am quite looking forward to seeing Heir Hyland's ambitious plans," the man said, grinning. "Making *Our Book of God* is such exciting business, even for someone my age. I'm expecting great things from you, too, Sir Col."

"You are too kind."

It was truly how he felt, not any sort of modesty, but the man cackled.

"For now, we will take care of everyone's stay at the Debau Company trading house. I will ensure all the necessary tools are in order as well."

"Thank you."

"Well, I must be off to my next destination. Once I hop onto my boat, I'll be at the next town. Heir Hyland should be arriving at Atiph by sea already. May God watch over you."

The man smiled slightly and left the room.

Standing in front of the closed door, Col heaved a deep sigh. Apparently he had been unconsciously nervous.

He knew he was simply one of many collaborators and that this was a real problem regarding faith. Despite that, he felt something burning deep within his chest—the pope, who had forgotten his original duty, and the Kingdom of Winfiel, which stood up to challenge him.

He did not think he had ever felt the excitement of facing a major task and the yearning for adventure in him.

First, he decided that even if it was too presumptuous of him to want to be Hyland's support in Atiph, he would help somehow. Then—

"Oh! Brother!"

His somber thoughts shattered when he heard Myuri's silly voice from the other side of the door.

"Open up!"

There came the *thud, thud* of kicks against the door.

41

He sighed and opened it.

"How many times have I told you to stop kicking the door?"

"Ah! Ah! Move, move!"

Myuri listened to none of Col's scolding and stumbled into the room, bumping into him in the process. Her arms were stuffed with things that somehow did not fall onto the floor, and she eventually managed to place them on the bed.

"My hands, they're so hot! I think I burned them…"

She blew hard onto them, but Col stood still, dumbfounded.

"Myuri? Why do you have so many things?"

He had given her bronze *dip* pieces, the area's smallest currency in circulation. Two or three were enough to buy one meal, so they were perfect for buying a few slices of pork and old, dried bread.

With that, Myuri had acquired a variety of things wrapped in big leaves and three fine pieces of bread as thick as her thighs. No matter how he figured it, that was much more than what the money could buy. To top it off, she even had a small wine cask.

"I thought I told you no alcohol."

Myuri pouted, as though it was too much trouble to keep ignoring him.

"I didn't buy it."

"You didn't?"

"They gave it to me."

"That's not—Wait, all of this?"

Then, Myuri suddenly smiled proudly.

"I was waiting for the pig to roast, and they asked me to come dancing. When I danced along to the music everyone was so happy!"

She placed her hands on her cheeks, and when she spun around merrily, her ears and tail appeared. She was a girl who enjoyed any sort of festivities and often joined the dancers at the bathhouse in Nyohhira.

42

Col watched her and sighed, his hand meeting his forehead. Then, while she pranced about, humming and flicking her bushy tail, he stopped her by pressing on her head.

"Myuri, from now on, you must be more careful about these things."

"Huh?"

Underneath his hand, a puzzled Myuri looked up at him.

Then, she opened her mouth as though she realized something.

"Ah...Um, I did think that, maybe, um, getting on the table with my shoes on was a bad thing, but..."

Her ears drooped, and her tail hung lifelessly.

Col felt light-headed—she had done such a thing?

"But...but...I checked to see if there were other dancers! I know I shouldn't get in the way of their work!"

She confidently puffed up her chest as if to declare that she knew that much.

When she would join the circle of performers in Nyohhira, she shone the brightest with her cheerfulness and innocence.

But then, instead of tipping the true dancers and perhaps receiving a small smile in return, the guests started giving meat and bread to the innocent Myuri to watch her wolf it down. It became a major infringement on the dancers' territory, and she had caused man disputes. She was likely alluding to that. Col let go of her head, made a fist, and lightly rapped her with it.

"That is not what I'm talking about."

"...?"

Myuri dramatically pressed a hand to her head in objection.

Suddenly exhausted, Col opened the window and gazed out, knowing that there used to be a time when she actually listened to him.

"This is not Nyohhira. It's dangerous for a girl to dance in front of drunkards."

The roasting pig from earlier was now nothing but bone. The guests had drunk quite a bit and were amusing themselves with arm wrestling at the moment.

The usual gathering at this checkpoint was comprised of merchants buying and selling furs or timber, those who transported cargo, and the captains who steered the ships. All things considered, the crowd was a bit rough, but it was not on the level of mercenaries.

"Dangerous?" Myuri repeated the word as a question, dubious.

"That means not every man will drop to one knee and hold out flowers after they've had their heart stolen by a wonderful dance."

And Myuri appeared defenseless enough as it was.

"Oh, that's what you mean. It's okay!" Myuri said as she reached out for the food she had thrown onto the bed. She undid the carefully wound leaf wrapping around what appeared to be truly delicious-looking pork, still dripping fat.

"Miss Helen taught me lots. And Mother also said that the value of a woman depends on how many men she's declined," she said while pinching the pork and putting it into her mouth before licking the fat off her fingers.

Myuri had spent time with the children of nobles on occasion, and once they tired of hunting in the mountains, there was nothing else to do. Whether they were joking or not, many called out to her.

It was normal for her to receive men's attention. If he scolded her, warning that she would never get married if she continued like this, she would not listen.

"Honestly..."

Perhaps it was that girls her age were not afraid of anything.

He suddenly felt as though he had aged ten, twenty years and said, "Not everyone is reasonable."

As she ate her second piece of meat, Myuri slumped, indicating that perhaps his lecturing was finally sinking in.

"It would already be too late if something had happened to you. Do you understand, Myuri? You are still young and ignorant of the world. When I tell you to be more careful, it's not because I'm teasing you, but because it's how I can protect you."

As he explained fluently to the girl in front of him, Myuri placed the package of meat on the bed, ripped open the bread, and placed the meat between the pieces.

She was bent over as she did so, and her fluffy ashen tail swished back and forth behind her small bottom. It was as though she was reassuring him—*It's all right, it's all right.*

"Are you listening to me?"

"Yeeep. Here, this one is for you."

With a smile, she offered him an enormous piece of bread that was, of course, as big as her thigh. Plenty of meat was sandwiched inside of it, as well as cheese to stuff it full.

"...I can't eat all this."

"What? But, Brother, that's why you're too skinny."

"S-skinny..."

Though he was not quite on the level of hunters and mercenaries, Col thought he had enough muscle on him, so that remark stung considerably.

And the piece of bread that Myuri took for herself was much bigger than the one she had handed him, and he felt full just from looking at it.

"Digging in!"

Myuri opened her mouth wide and bit aggressively into the bread. Her ears and tail wiggled in bliss—where did she find room for everything in that slender body of hers?

"Good grief..."

Col did not know how many times he had sighed that day. He watched Myuri engrossed in her meal before taking a bite of bread himself. It would be a lie to say that he was not, in a way, jealous of how she saw the world as brimming with exciting things, beautiful vistas, smiles and happiness.

Though that did not mean he wanted her to lose her innocence and regard others with a doubtful eye. Nothing would be better than if he could raise her to be as straightforward as this, without anything ever hurting her.

To that end, he wanted her to know as little of the outside world as possible and live quietly in Nyohhira.

"And we need to talk about you going back to Nyohhira."

When he broached the subject, Myuri suddenly stopped munching on the bread and tilted her head to the side in annoyance.

"Don't play dumb with me," he said.

Surely, Myuri was not foolish enough to think that he would accept their traveling together just like that.

Just as he expected, when he pointed this out to her, her expression changed and she tore into the bread. It seemed her laudable attitude had existed only on the boat.

"No, I'm not going back."

"Yes, you are."

When he cut her down with a single stroke, her tail bristled.

"I planned on taking you to Svernel, where we would find someone trustworthy to bring you back, but my plans have changed. Tomorrow morning, I will send a fast horse with a letter to Nyohhira and have someone come to get you."

During this time of year, there were many guests in every bathhouse, and it was very busy. This thought alone made him want to take her home himself, but trudging back along the snowy mountain roads with Myuri in tow would take two or three days.

He needed to move forward quickly now that Hyland, who had hired him directly, might already be in Atiph.

"And Lawrence and Holo must be worrying about you back in Nyohhira right about now."

It would be odd if Lawrence were not growing frantic now. Or perhaps, Myuri's mother, Holo, would come under the cover of darkness in her true form, a giant beast known as the wisewolf who could swallow a person whole.

Actually, that would make Col more than happy since Myuri only ever obeyed her mother.

But just as the thought occurred to him—

"They're not," Myuri said, a hint of desperation in her voice. Perhaps it was typical for someone her age to see her parents' meddling as annoying. She might rebel if he admonished her directly, so he wondered how to lecture her. As he searched his memory for a passage from the scriptures, Myuri held a piece of bread in her mouth, spread her hands, and then pulled something out from under her shirt.

"*Ehho-hey, ah-hoo, hee-how-ha-how, ha-haw-ha-haw.*"

"I'm sorry, what did you say?"

As Col asked, he noticed what she had drawn from her clothing.

"Hmm…Ah, that's—!"

Myuri was not desperate—she was exasperated.

She was holding a small pouch tied together by a string. It was nothing special at a glance, but it was enough to make him fall silent.

"*Ehho…Nom, gulp.* There's no way I could leave the house without Mother knowing."

That pouch belonged to Myuri's mother, Holo. It was small

enough to fit comfortably in a fist, and Holo always had it around her neck. That was because it was stuffed with different kinds of wheat inside, and Holo lived in the grains as a being who had once controlled its harvest.

"When I told Mother about you, she put some wheat in the pouch and gave it to me. She said to take care of you and that if I have this, I can protect you when the time is right."

When he heard that, he felt as though heaven and earth had been flipped.

Not him looking after Myuri but Myuri looking after him?

She stared right at him as he stood in a daze.

"What were you talking about just now?"

Her gaze chilled him to his core.

"Just now?"

It was not necessarily revenge, but when he responded dumbly, the fur on Myuri's tail stood on end.

"You met with a stranger here!"

"You eavesdropped..."

"You were inside talking when I came back so I was just waiting outside!" So she said, but she had definitely strained her wolf ears to listen in. "But that doesn't matter! You are going to go to some faraway land to be a priest! I knew it! You liar!"

She bared her canines, which stood out a bit more than the average human's, perhaps because of her wolf's blood, and growled loudly. The fur on her tail, too, bristled like a ragged brush.

He had told Lawrence and Holo, the bathhouse owners, the true reason for his journey. However, he had figured Myuri would not understand if he explained it to her since it could get complicated, so he simply told her that he would be going to help an acquaintance someplace far away.

"That blondie is tricking you!"

Hyland had beautiful, eye-catching blond hair, as was appropriate for someone with royal blood.

Myuri, for some reason, regarded him with blind hostility. She was attached to the mysterious mixture of ash and silver that was her own hair, so perhaps she regarded him as an enemy.

"I am not being tricked. What Heir Hyland is doing is very important."

"Yes, you are. You're too softhearted, and people can lure you into anything!"

He would take the "softhearted" part as a compliment. "Then, how do you think I am being tricked?" Col retorted, biting into the meal Myuri had made for him. If he told that fireball everything without giving her a chance, he would be the one tiring out. As with his lectures, he had no choice but to let her talk and talk and confuse herself before she would give in.

That was also how he had dealt with her vicious attacks this past week.

But Myuri, too, was likely getting a feel for this strategy. As she glared at him, munching on her bread, she appeared to be building up her strength.

"*Aughm, nom...gulp.* You are. Because it's weird! That blondie is a powerful person in the kingdom or whatever, right? So why would someone like that go to you for help?"

Col was aware that he was naturally meek, and he was proud of his modesty. Myuri had pointed that out with this in mind, and he knew he should simply accept it, but of course, certain things he could not budge on.

"The scholars and high-ranking clergy who come to Nyohhira have always regarded me highly. You may not think so, but—" It was embarrassing for him to sing his own praises, but he had no choice. "—but they're right."

"Hmph."

Myuri regarded him with narrowed eyes and then snorted. They were not the eyes of the little sister who wagged her tail innocently and called out to him, "Brother, Brother!"

They were the same eyes as a dancer who was rather harsh with men watching an intoxicated guest's loud boasting.

"Um, Brother? Even I know the visiting priests are important people. Important people have dignity, and that's what makes them great. You're not like them."

Those were the words of a child who had never left her village deep in the mountains.

"*Sigh*...Listen, Myuri. There is an account of this in the scripture. God bestowed his words onto a prophet, who returned to the village where he was born. His relatives said to him: 'You do not hesitate to say that God has given his word to you, but we ask that you must stop such exaggerations. We know that you have always been a normal child.' Then, the prophet said to his disciples: 'Take something in your hand and bring it close to your eyes. The closer you are, the less you can see of its true shape.'"

The scripture was full of meaning from this perspective. As Col mulled over the words, Myuri spoke.

"But there are also things that you can only see because you're close!"

"...For example?" Col replied with a question, sighing.

Myuri's eyes glinted coolly.

"When Miss Helen and the other dancing girls tease you, your face immediately goes red and you get all flustered."

"Wha—?"

A dagger of ice came flying at him from a completely unexpected direction.

"Whenever I see it I think how there's really nothing sadder than that. You know a lot about the scripture, Brother, but does the scripture teach you how to talk to girls?"

The dagger plunged deep into his chest and twisted mercilessly.

While his breath was failing him, Myuri bit into what was left of her bread, chewing in disappointment.

"The older guests know how to treat girls, for that matter. They seem to know when to act shy, and that actually makes them more attractive. I think that's what makes someone an important person."

Even those who were rather learned and well versed when it came to theology were just old men when they soaked in the waters of Nyohhira and ogled the half-naked dancers. He could not bring himself to bring it up with them directly, but he had no way of knowing how many "nieces" and "nephews" these men had despite their supposed celibacy.

So Col secretly thought that since he adhered to his abstinence, there was no mistaking that he would achieve much greater things than them. However, Myuri's assessment was the opposite.

"Mother says this a lot to Father." Myuri cleared her throat and imitated her mother, Holo. "You act like you understand everything about the world, but you shall never see more than half if you do not understand women! There is nothing in this world but women and men!"

His chest was in so much pain he felt faint, and that was when Myuri landed the finishing blow.

"And, Brother, have you even held hands with another girl besides me?"

Col was about to protest that he had at least done that, but the first person who came to mind was Myuri's mother, Holo. And Holo was a mother figure, not just for Myuri but for Col as well. If he argued that he had held hands with Holo, Myuri would roll on the floor laughing and perhaps regard him with some worry.

However, he could not leave the question unanswered. He raised his own spirits by reassuring himself that what he wanted to accomplish was much too complicated to be comprehended by a little girl.

"Wh-whatever the case, I believe that Heir Hyland—and by extension, the Kingdom of Winfiel—are in the right, so I decided to go on a journey where I could be of some help to them. And I would rather be unacquainted with the opposite sex. The vows of abstinence will only strengthen my faith!"

He became defiant—no one could understand this pride. In reality, vows of abstinence were the butt of ridicule, and priests who kept to them were few and far between.

But Col was all right with that. He could not die for his faith, so how could he keep moving forward?

"That is why—"

Just as he was about to speak to Myuri, she quickly stuffed the rest of the bread in her mouth, licked her fingers, and interrupted him.

"That's why I have to stay by your side."

"Ah...What?"

"Mother was worried, too. She said you're super-reliable, but since girls are a weakness of yours, you might get roped into something troublesome. She said it would be awful if you came back to Nyohhira all proud of yourself with some weird girl, after you finished your work."

"..."

"Mother's worried that Father might be conned by someone, so she won't leave Nyohhira. That means I'll be with you because I'm the one who needs to keep an eye on you," Myuri said with a grin.

He wondered why he found that smile so frightening, and the

answer was because she was the spitting image of her mother, Holo. The wisewolf would often laugh like this as she amused herself treating Lawrence, a top-class merchant who had participated in the tumult that irrevocably changed the northlands ten years ago, as if he were a child.

Myuri swished her tail back and forth, like a wolf watching its prey try to escape.

Col gulped, and Myuri slid closer.

"And I'm worried about you, too, Brother. I'm serious."

There was more than a head's difference in height between them, so when Myuri stood next to Col, she only reached his chest.

She gazed up at him with wide eyes.

The magic of it scattered the words of the sentence he was about to say, but he somehow kept himself grounded in reality. Bread crumbs and bits of cheese stuck goofily to her lips.

"…First, wipe your mouth."

"Huh? Oh."

She hurriedly wiped her mouth with her sleeve. Then, when she glanced at him, her smile seemed like an attempt to hide that her mischief had been found out.

"You're growing up to be an odd person…"

He hung his head, and Myuri stood on her tiptoes to pat him.

"Shh, shh, it's okay. Mother told me to look after you. Leave it to me."

"…"

She was half his age. He heard her cries when she was born; he had often changed her diapers. Countless times, she had crawled under the covers with him so that she did not get frostbite during the winter months, only to wet the bed and start sobbing while he soothed her and cleaned up.

That girl had, at some point, become this.

Of course, her mother was a master of the weapon known as womanhood, so it was natural that her daughter be the same.

He wished he could speak with Lawrence about it.

"So I can travel with you, right?"

He was unsure why she was suddenly speaking so lightheartedly, but he was well aware that he was no match for her when Holo was on her side.

And Myuri knew exactly what she needed to.

"Of course, I won't bother you. I don't know anything about God."

That was certainly a problem, but perhaps Myuri, with the blood of ancient spirits flowing through her veins, had the right to disregard a God whose existence was not certain.

"But I'll be sure to point out anything you miss straight away, my careless Brother."

He wanted to check to see where that confidence came from, but it was likely because she had the blood of a wolf, the ruler of the forest.

"Oh, and, Brother?"

"…What is it?" he responded with fatigue, as Myuri hesitantly pointed at something.

"Do you still want that?"

She was pointing at his half-eaten food, and he sighed.

"Go ahead."

He handed it to her, and she bit into it happily, even though she had just finished a large piece. As Col watched her, he could not help the defeated smile spreading on his face.

And once it did, he lost.

"Haa-haw?" ("What's wrong?") Myuri asked, her mouth stuffed with bread, and Col patted her head before pointing to a chair.

"Sit down and eat."

Myuri quietly obeyed and plopped down onto the chair.

Her apparent obedience at times like these was another of her crafty tricks. He understood it all.

"Oh God, please grant me strength…"

As he chanted the name of his eternal companion, he sighed.

CHAPTER TWO

The following day, Col awoke before dawn. It was the time of night when the moon still shone brightly and the mountain air was at its coldest.

Those around him often praised him for being a hard worker who did not mind waking up early, but the truth was, he was sleepy. To him, it was all for show. As he mentally reviewed the list of duties he had to do today at the bathhouse, he realized something odd.

Outside, he could hear voices and footsteps on gravel.

And above him was an unfamiliar ceiling, and he was in a different bed.

"...Ah."

He remembered that he had left on a journey.

Then, when he moved to get up, he realized there was another person in the bed. It was Myuri, who only behaved when she was asleep. He had put her to sleep in the other bed, so she must have switched during the night.

It was hot under the covers, thanks to her body heat and fluffy tail.

They had argued over this and that last night, and the reason

59

Myuri wanted to travel was most likely because she was bored of the village. Though she worried about him with some reluctance, the worry itself was real.

Her silver hair looked strangely dewy even though it was not wet or oiled. If he ran his hands through it, the strands would slip through his fingers. Holo was proud of the beautiful lay of the fur on her tail, but Myuri's pride came from this color that she inherited from her father.

As he stroked her head, her animal ears twitched. But there was no sign of her waking. She probably would not wake up if he shook her shoulders. He smiled slightly and got out from under the blanket.

He opened the window, and it was cold enough outside to freeze his breath, though there was no wind or snow.

There were already people moving about in the square, which had been busy late into the night, and the riverbeds beyond it. They were probably heading out to catch the morning markets in the watershed towns.

He closed the shutters, put on his coat, took his scripture in hand, and went down to the first floor. The ice in the back well had already been broken, so he scooped up some water into a tub and washed his face and brushed his teeth with the smashed end of a tree branch, then did his daily recitation of the scripture. Other guests came to wash their faces as he did so, and they took advantage of the situation by bowing their heads to his recitation, taking it as protection for the road. It was like catching rain in a tub, but he did not dislike the frank practicality of the merchants.

The problem was that even though he did his recitations for longer than usual, the sun still had not risen, and he had no work to do afterward. He grew bored, and that troubled him slightly.

In the end, since it would also be a waste to do nothing, he headed to the riverside and helped with the loading and unloading of cargo. When the sky began to lighten, he returned to the room.

"You work too much, brother…"

He finally managed to wake Myuri, who could sleep through any disturbance, and when he recounted all he had done so far, she fussed about his excessive zeal.

Though she sat up straight, her eyes would not open because of how tired she was. She hugged her tail for warmth and yawned loudly.

"This is what it means to travel with me. Are you giving up?"

Her ears stood up straight as she struggled to open her eyes.

"N-no fair!"

"It is fair. All right, put your ears and tail away and wash your face. Get ready quickly or I'll leave you behind."

"Sheesh!"

She puffed up her cheeks and tail, then retrieved a handkerchief and other things from her bag. Upon closer inspection, there were two combs and three brushes. He could not see what she needed so many for. As he pondered questions more difficult than those of theology, Myuri left the room with an odd parting comment.

"I'm going to groom my hair in the baths."

When he turned toward her, the door had already closed.

Then, before long, she came running back in.

"B-Brother, where are the baths?!"

"The baths?"

"Th-there's nothing but a well, and…and when I looked inside, th-there was ice in it…I can't wash my hair without the baths!"

Myuri was half in tears, and like a priest hearing a profound complaint, Col lifted his head. After that, he nodded slowly as if he deeply agreed.

Hot spring water bubbled up everywhere in Nyohhira, to the

61

point that it was disposable. Myuri was born and raised there. There were many stories of noble girls who left their manors for the first time and discovered how blessed they had been, but he did not imagine such a tale would play out before his eyes.

It would be a lie to say he did not gain a slightest sadistic enjoyment from it.

"There are no baths here. This isn't Nyohhira."

"Oh…"

"Is this too hard? If it is, then you can…"

"I won't quit! I won't!"

Myuri declared her intentions and, with wide strides, stomped back out into the hallway.

It was a strength of hers that she was not easily discouraged, at least.

The hair care that the dancer Helen told Myuri about consisted of the following: After combing the hair out, go over it carefully with a long-haired brush and a short-haired brush, both made from the mane of a horse, and then a brush made of pig's hair. Col thought it odd that so much brushing did not instead damage the hair, but at any rate, it was practically self-harm for Myuri to wash her hair while it was so cold out.

When she returned to the room, her lips were blue, and she was shivering.

"…Honestly."

He removed his overcoat and covered her with it.

"And while you were performing ablutions outside, a letter came."

Out of some respect, he used the term "ablutions" for her willpower to wash her hair in ice water simply for appearances' sake. He, of course, also meant it sarcastically, so she eyed him spitefully.

"Wh-wh...what...*achoo!* L-letter?"

"It seems to have come by boat from Nyohhira."

It apparently could not reach them the night before, so it spent the night at a checkpoint farther upstream and came on the first vessel out that morning. A considerable amount of money had been paid for its delivery, so the captain who brought it mistook the missive for an important, confidential letter of a noble.

"It's from Lawrence...and Holo."

He opened the letter, read the inside, and could not help a wry smile. Myuri, curled up inside the coat that was clearly much too big for her, tilted her head like a kitten. Col handed the letter to her, and she made an unreadable smile. Though it had taken extraordinary effort to teach her, she was able to read to a certain extent as a result.

In the letter, there were countless spelling mistakes to show that Lawrence was panicking as he asked about Myuri's safety, stating that he would go get her as soon as possible, but a large *X* had been mercilessly drawn over it.

Then, something else was written in the margin with unique handwriting.

"'T-take care of,' Broth...*Achoo!*"

"It says, 'Take care of Myuri,'" he responded with a sigh, and Myuri returned the letter, sniffling and teeth chattering. "I was slightly hoping they would stop you."

Holo had brushed aside Lawrence's opinions, though he was the head of the household. This family would certainly be one of strong women.

"Spare the rod and spoil the ch...*Hachoo!*"

He looked at Myuri, and after she sniffled, a wide grin that displayed her canines appeared on her face.

"I'm the one who should be spared."

Myuri was about to protest when she sneezed loudly again.

After writing a response to Lawrence and Holo, they ate the previous night's leftovers as breakfast. They left a letter with the innkeeper, finished their preparations, and headed to the riverside. A fire was still blazing there, so Myuri dried her damp hair. Passing boatmen smiled at the sight, thinking she had fallen into the well.

They bargained around to find a vessel to take them to Atiph, and eventually they struck a deal to travel on a boat loaded with firewood, chickens, and other cargo for scheduled deliveries to towns along the way. It had little space for carrying passengers, which the captain treated as a side job, so it was nowhere near a comfortable ride.

But the sun finally rose and warmed their bodies, and Myuri, who had been preening herself like a little bird beside him, was napping, perhaps out of boredom. It was pleasant.

He could imagine what was happening in the bathhouse right about now and who was doing what. Perhaps this was what it meant for Col to leave the life he had led for more than ten years. And though he had promised Myuri he would come back in order to soothe her, there was also a good possibility that he would not. Lawrence and Holo had sent him off understanding that. He could only be thankful to have met such good people.

As he sat consumed with his thoughts, the boat sailed downstream. The current was gentle, and the river was wide. This journey of two, which had happened so completely against his will, ended its second day without event, and the third day was the same.

Myuri also wanted to wash her hair on the morning of the third day, but she had learned her lesson to some extent and came up with the idea of first boiling water in the inn's kitchen. However, she also made the shocking discovery that she would need money for fuel and coal. Maybe she had never imagined that it cost money to have hot water.

In the end, she washed her hair in a half-frozen well, but this time she adjusted her approach and finished with minimal shivering. He was looking forward to seeing what she would try next time.

Before long, the stones on the riverbed grew fewer in number, and the grassland views became more frequent. Gently sloping plains stretched out all the way to the mountains that were faintly visible in the distance. It seemed they had reached the Dolan Plains. Col became drowsy watching the scenery, but it was terribly exciting for Myuri, who had grown up high in the mountains. She excitedly stared at the view and waved to the travelers walking along the riverside roads.

Then finally, beyond the sloping plains, the town of Atiph came into view atop a small hill, along with its famous checkpoint.

"...!!"

It was difficult just to keep Myuri from suddenly standing up in the boat, so Col was worried that her ears and tail might come out. She gave a wordless cry in enthusiasm, and he had trouble gently prying off her tight grip on his arm.

"Brother! The town! So big! The river! It's true! The chain!"

It was like she forgot how to form full sentences in her excitement.

But he was genuinely surprised to see the very thing their other captain had described, looming over them with more presence than he had imagined. It was not the kind of chain that was used to keep vaults closed—each link was big enough that Myuri could fit her arm through it. Each joint was lined up neatly and the chain hung above the pair.

"C-captain! Are you sure it won't fall?" Myuri asked, having

regained some composure, and the captain, with sloping shoulders and a mustache under his nose, spoke without a smile.

"It falls once a year, and the boats get caught in it and sink. It hasn't fallen yet this year, so we're still in danger. Can you swim?"

Myuri's face twitched, and she clung to Col, then peered up at the chain.

"She will believe you, so please don't tease her."

"Wha—?"

Myuri was shocked, and the captain laughed.

"Can you see the nests the birds of passage leave in the links?" Col pointed, and Myuri's mouth fell open as the chain passed directly above them. "If it fell and the water washed it clean every year, it would not be like that."

"The chain doesn't fall, but shit does all the time. You're putting yourself in danger looking up with your mouth open."

Myuri quickly shut her mouth when she heard the captain's warning.

Their boat joined many others and headed for the pier. There were too many of them, so they had to wait their turn. Everyone was unloading here and seemed to be bringing back a mountain of salted herring in return. When they finally reached the pier, Myuri wearily watched the loading of the fish onto the boats.

"I'm so glad I'm not with the fish. I don't even want to look at salted fish anymore."

Herring was abundant, so it was cheap. During the winter, it was laid out on every table in every house from the coast to the mountains and elicited considerable moaning. This was the fish that kept them fed every winter, and it would be distributed at every cargo ship's next stop.

"Well, the smell is already bad…"

Myuri must have been having a bad time, since her good sense of smell was due to her wolf's blood. Even for a regular person

67

like Col, he could clearly smell the fishy scent wafting from the barrels here and there in the port.

Though this time, he could only think of how delicious it smelled.

"Let's have salt-grilled fish tonight. It's a different kind of taste from salted fish."

"Aww...I wanted red meat..."

Myuri grumbled in disapproval of their journey's meals as they cut through the crowds at the pier and exited the port, but then she suddenly became quiet.

"What's wrong?"

Col glanced at her, and she was gaping up at the sky. She stared at the stone fortress with seabirds lined up snugly on it. It was the first time she had ever seen a town outside Nyohhira in her life.

"Myuri, you'll be in the way if you stop there."

He pulled her hand, and she finally moved, but something else immediately stole her attention.

"Brother, look! That person has so many dogs!" She pointed to a dockhand carrying a barrel, and the pack of dogs following behind him. "Is that a dog herder?"

"Dog herder?"

"There are goatherds and shepherds all over the world, right?"

Following that logic, of course there would be dog herders somewhere in the world.

"I don't know much about dog herders, but that barrel probably has salted herring in it. The dogs are after the salt that might spill out."

"Ohhh."

Seabirds circled noisily above Myuri as she stood in wonder, and a cat curled up on a stack of wooden crates. Everything was new and exciting in the commotion of the port, and she busied herself asking what this and that was with each step she took.

Then, her eyes sparkled whenever she heard the answer, and she listened enthusiastically to his every word. And though she had grown cheeky lately, seeing her like this reminded Col of the straightforward and cute Myuri from so long ago, and so he relaxed.

However, explaining every little thing would not get them anywhere, and they still had preparations to make upon entering the town. First, they had to find a money changer to ensure they had cash to do shopping in town. When he finally decided to pull her along so that they could move forward—and since he was trying to get a hold of Myuri, he was not watching where he was going—they ran into someone.

"Oh, I'm sorry."

Flustered, he apologized to a girl wearing a kerchief around her head. She was relatively tall, and slender arms extended from her emphatically rolled-up sleeves. She was wearing an apron, so perhaps she was the daughter of a shipping agent. Her pale hair, faded from the salt of the sea, matched her particularly beautiful chestnut-colored eyes.

Her gaze met Col's, and she smiled. But out of the blue, she quickly latched onto his arm.

"Not at all! I welcome good-looking people like you!"

"Huh?"

"You're a traveler, right? Is this your first time to the town of Atiph? Do you have an inn for the night? If you loiter around here, the touts from nasty inns will drag you in."

"Wh-what? Um—"

She rambled to him about so much all at once, and suddenly the girl's chest touched his arm. Her supple flesh had received a splendid upbringing in the spirit of meat, fish, and the seaside.

"Our inn is clean and safe. We've just unloaded some new wine, our beds have marvelous linen without any mites or lice, and any girl you choose will be yours. What, priests like yourself are fine, too! All the girls are the devout lambs of God, so God will overlook this. So just get married for a night and then divorce the next day."

"Th-that's, um…"

Col knew immediately that it was the kind of inn that provided companionship with a girl in exchange for money. Any port town, teeming with famously boisterous sailors and the rich who gained all their money from trade, would have any number of these sorts of inns. The girl pressed her chest more firmly against his arm this time and drew close to his face as though she would whisper in his ear. He did not know what sort of incense she was burning, but he could smell the sweet scent of fresh bread. He could not look straight at the girl.

"Heh-heh, it's kind of cute when your face goes red like that. Hey, where did you come from? Did you come by boat from the south? Tell me all about your journey at the inn," the girl said and tried to pull him along by his arm. *No, I am not a priest, and we have plans to stay at a different inn*—his words echoed vainly in his head.

All the same, when he tried to stand his ground, he felt his other arm being pulled in the other direction.

"See, our inn is over…Ah, huh?" The sheep she had caught did not budge, so she turned back toward him dubiously. "Oh, what, is that your daughter?"

He looked, and there was Myuri, hugging his other arm and glaring daggers at the girl.

"I've never seen you before. Whose turf are you from?"

The girl's expression changed from a pleasant one for customers to a dangerous one. She said "turf," which likely meant she thought that Myuri was in the same industry as she was. Myuri's outfit did not suggest she was the daughter of an honorable baker.

"N-no, this is the daughter of my employer, and we have reason to be traveling together," Col said before things became complicated. The girl stared, comparing herself and Myuri three times before she finally let go of his arm.

"The reason you smell so strongly of sulfur must mean you're headed home after plenty of fun in Nyohhira. I see."

She nodded all-knowingly, and there was no doubt she was mistaken, but it would be too much trouble to correct her.

"Then, don't worry about the inn, but could you exchange some money for me?"

"Exchange money?"

"Since you came down the river, you should have small coins, right?"

The tout girl changed the subject suddenly, and Col grew a bit flustered.

"We're having trouble since we don't have enough change. Of course, I'll give you a little something for the exchange fees. Like a kiss on the cheek or letting you lay your head on my lap..."

And again, she slid closer to him, and Myuri literally growled.

"It's a joke. But really, could you give me just a little? We're really in a bind."

She probably spoke to clueless travelers like this to cheat them out of change at an unfair rate.

"I'm sorry. We were just going to the money changers ourselves," he informed her, and she did not pursue the matter further. "I see. Then you shouldn't get money changed outside the city walls. The ones without a mat aren't licensed, you know. They'll overcharge you so much, so be careful. You seem too honest...Well, you have a little supervisor with you."

The girl cackled, and as Myuri gave her a little wave, she turned on her heels. She no longer had any interest in them as she looked around and purposefully bumped into a different passing young man. He seemed honest and kind, perhaps coming into town from one of the nearby farming villages.

Their conversation was the same as the one Col had earlier, and just as the young man was about to apologize, she pressed her chest against his arm and drew her face close to his ear. Col and Myuri could easily tell from the side that this honest-looking young man was freezing up.

This method was not often praised, but Col admired her enthusiastic salesmanship and wit.

"I swear!" There echoed a cold, sharp voice. "You really can't do anything without me."

He turned around to see Myuri's exasperated expression. Col once again turned his gaze to the young man—the girl would not hear his confused excuses. She gripped his arm, then simply dragged him off. The weak would be hunted.

"And you were all blushy!"

"I wasn't b-*blushy*,"Col retorted, flustered, but Myuri was eyeing him in disdain as she snorted.

"They were just a bit big."

"Huh?" he asked, and Myuri let go of his arm, instead taking his hand. Hers was a small hand and so was her height and her shoulders and her waist—many parts of her were small. Perhaps she had released him because she was embarrassed of what she had been pressing against his arm, especially compared to the other girl. Of course, he did not point any of this out and pretended not to notice.

Instead, he said, "But you did save me. I give you my thanks."

Displeased, Myuri stared up at Col before suddenly smiling, like a sign flipping upside down.

If they stood around idly, another predator might turn their fangs on them. Quickly, they walked off, and Myuri, generally satisfied after staring at the activity in the port, spoke up.

"And, Brother? What are you doing here? Preaching on a street corner?"

"No, I won't be doing that. For the most part, I'll be helping Heir Hyland."

"What was it? *Our Book of…*"

So she did overhear. There was no reason to hide it now.

"Our Book of God."

"What is that?"

"It's our plan to translate scripture into common language."

"Oh, I see," she said, though her expression suggested she did not see at all.

Col looked at her in shock, and she giggled in response.

"The scripture is written in the script of the Church. In ancient times, the words of the prophets were written down for posterity, but since the Church spread all over the world, very few priests were able to read the original script as a result. It's said that was when God granted us the script of the Church."

"Huh. How long ago is ancient times? Before Mother was a kid?"

Unwittingly, he glanced around, but he relaxed, doubting anyone would come and seriously question them.

"That is a good question. Perhaps it could be."

"Huh."

Her interest lay in an odd part of the story, but the main topic was elsewhere, so he cleared his throat and steered the conversation back.

"Anyway, the scripture is written in the orthography of the Church, but that's not what we usually use. Few can read and write even the common script we use every day."

Myuri made a disgusted face, likely recalling how she was sometimes roped to a chair, forced to learn how to read and write.

"Because of that, only a small number of people can read the scripture. So if you go to a church, the priest will interpret the teachings written in the scripture for you, and it's been this way for a very, very long time. However, lately, it's been agreed that this is not a good thing. So our plan is, instead of only the priests of the Church one-sidedly reading and interpreting the righteousness of God's teachings, we will enable many people to read the scripture directly, and each person will decide for themselves what is right."

"So *Our Book of God*?"

"Yes. Isn't that a wonderful name?"

Myuri stared at Col with those beautiful eyes, then spoke.

"Brother, you treat me like a child, but you're plenty childish yourself."

"What?" he asked in return, but she only smiled mischievously.

Although, it was true that *Our Book of God* would be filled with the elements of adventure and challenge, enough to make his nostrils flare with enthusiasm.

"So you're going to write a book."

"Frankly speaking."

However, translating the scripture was easier said than done. It was brimming with vague and metaphoric language, and interpretations differed from one theological scholar to the next. In addition, there was a lot of jargon that was not used in daily life, so translating it would not be straightforward.

What was more, Col was aware of the reality that devout faith was not the only force driving their plan forward. It was nothing if not a strategic maneuver, born from the current standoff between the pope and the Kingdom of Winfiel that had continued for too long. It was a way for the kingdom to prove that the pope was wrong and to cut his feet out from under him. As anyone could clearly see, when he held the scripture in one hand and glorified asceticism in front of a magnificent cathedral with a giant bell tower, what he preached and what he practiced were different. However, since the people could not read the scripture, it was difficult, if not impossible, for them to point out his misdeeds.

Of course, it was clear that the Church strongly opposed their plan. As long as the scripture was not written in a common language, they could limit the number of people who could access it, and they could keep the uneducated masses ignorant. *Our Book of God* was a plan that would give the Church quite the headache.

Yet, on the Kingdom of Winfiel's side of things, there was an earnest and practical reason for undertaking this plan. Since church doors had been ordered closed all throughout the country, the government had to give people the power to conduct baptisms, weddings, and prayers for funerals on their own.

Hyland, who came up with the plan for *Our Book of God*, really did have keen insight. The reason the Debau Company decided to support the kingdom was likely due to his intelligence.

However, it was also fair to say that this was the last resort of a cornered people. The suspension of all religious activities was a terrifying measure. As a loved one lay expiring on their deathbed, even if one wished to pray for their passage into heaven themselves, only a priest could do that. One could not receive God's blessings for their joyous wedding, an event that marked a major turning point in anyone's life. The Church was the one that carried out weddings, so no one could even get married officially in the first place. The pope had annulled all of it simply due to his desire to collect taxes. What did he even think of others' lives? God's love was free; his teachings were not for collecting tithes.

Col thought that yes, it was the pope who was wrong. If they condoned his tyranny, all that they believed was right in the world, and God himself, the root of that righteousness, would be taken from them.

"Brother."

As he mentally conversed with himself, Myuri pulled on his sleeve.

"You look scary."

"…I was thinking. What is it?"

"The port ends here. Where are we going? That town on the hill?"

The area around the port was much more developed than the town in the distance and contained numerous large buildings. There were warehouses that were also trading companies or shipping agents. The structures continued behind them, and beyond the paths were clusters of questionable shops where the girl from earlier pulled the young man to. And just as she said, some people were standing on the street corners, no mat beneath them, exchanging money. There were also blacksmiths' and woodcutters' workshops, so the port could already be called its own town.

However, they could see the size of the town from where they stood at the beginning of the paved road leading from the port up the hill. Scaffolding was set up here and there along the wall, so it seemed it was still expanding.

If the Debau Company had a trading house in Atiph, it would be there.

"Let's go into town."

"Yay!"

"Yay?"

He gave Myuri a questioning look. She turned away, but he knew what she was thinking.

"We will not be shopping or eating."

"Aww…But I saved you from a predator!"

"Th-that's…I refused as well myself."

He cleared his throat, and Myuri cheekily shrugged.

"First of all, we do not have infinite funds."

"I could earn money by dancing in a bar."

He glared at her, and she simply shrugged again, moving one step away from him. It was likely that she actually could earn money that way, and that bothered him.

"Luxury is the enemy."

"I think abstinence is the enemy of a fun life."

He glared again, but this time she smiled back.

The sides of the road from the port to the city walls were already packed with stalls.

On the path of trials given to the prophets by God, the temptations of the devil lay at every step.

Oh God, grant me protection.

He braced himself and swore again his vows of abstinence.

Atiph was a lively town, but it was a different sort from Nyohhira.

Loud shouts rose from anyone and everyone—as lively as if they were all running at full speed.

"Hey, get outta the way!"

"Who the hell put these crates here?!"

"Herring! Come get your herring! Fresh, unsalted herring!"

"You there, Mr. Traveler! How about a short sword to protect yourself? This masterpiece could even slice through a cow!"

Col had thought he was knowledgeable about the outside world, but it hit him that what he knew was from more than ten years in the past. Such hustle and bustle made him dizzy.

"Myuri, are you all right?"

The crowd jostled them about, stifling them with the heat of so many bodies, and the smells of fish and blood from the butchered sheep and pigs on the side of the streets wafted around them, as did the scent of the meat deep-frying in oil while the smoke of charcoal fires filled the air.

He worriedly called out to her, just when she had finished eating fried eel.

"Heh?" she responded, jumping out of the way of a cart loaded with cages that were stuffed with chickens, and patted a passing dog on the head as she spun. It seemed it did not take her very long to get used to the excitement of the town.

"Ooh! I want to eat that next!"

She pointed at a shop displaying its meat pies.

"…Fried eel from the mouth of the river, black pudding, tripe, what's next?"

"The small fried crabs were really good with salt. The fresh salt-grilled herring was better than I thought it would be. Herring isn't just something to throw out."

He was ashamed of himself for giving in to Myuri's pleading.

"Gluttony is one of the seven deadly sins. Do you know how much this cost? All the small change we brought from Nyohhira is gone now…"

It seemed every shop was short on change this time of year, and whenever he handed over a larger coin to pay, the owner showed a clear frown. Perhaps the tout girl had asked to exchange money not for extra savings, but truly because she was in a bind.

"We'll just do our shopping with silver, then. If we buy enough, we won't need any change."

"Myuri!" he scolded, and she stuck her fingers in her ears and averted her gaze.

"You should've gotten a farewell present from Father, so why are you being so stingy? If gluttony is a sin, then what about being such a miser?"

"Ah—"

She typically seemed to ignore his lectures, but since she did actually remember them, it would be hard to deal with her. Miserliness was not one of the seven deadly sins of wrath, gluttony, lust, greed, envy, pride, and sloth, but it was still sinful.

"…I am not being a miser. This is moderation."

"What's the difference?"

She was not asking because she did not know—she was asking because she knew it would trouble him. If her ears and tail had been out, they would probably have been wiggling happily.

Though it a shame for someone who wanted to be a priest, Col used his trump card.

"No means no."

Myuri blew a raspberry and turned away in a huff, but perhaps thinking it was time to stop, she did not harass him anymore.

Col evaluated the opportunity, then spoke.

"And you really must do something about your appearance."

"Huh?" Myuri had gone quiet, gazing around at the shops, wondering what to have him buy her tomorrow, and she sounded surprised. "What? Isn't it cute?"

She seemed slightly hurt.

"…This is not about whether it's cute or not."

"So? It is cute, right? Good."

She giggled happily, and he nearly gave in to her.

"It may look good on you." He tried again and managed to continue speaking. "But it stands out too much. If we are to continue traveling, you need to change. I'll get something else for you."

Myuri had a reason and an excuse for everything, but when he spoke with her seriously, she listened carefully.

She took another look at her outfit and tilted her head.

"If you insist, I'll change, but…why? Everyone compliments me!"

"That's why."

As with the tout girl's misunderstanding earlier, whenever Col paid for something Myuri bought at a stall, he could feel the gaze of the shopkeeper boring into him. He was walking around with a gaudily dressed girl who was young—perhaps too young—and buying her food. Perhaps it would be a different story if they were garish young nobles, but he had asked Lawrence for traveling clothes that were fitting for a priest. In no way was this respectable.

Col laid this out for Myuri in detail, and with a tired expression, she seemed to acquiesce.

"I don't care how others see me...but I don't want cause you trouble, Brother." Myuri sighed, then said, "So how should I dress?"

"Traveling women generally have two options for dress: a nun or a boy."

"Mother dresses like a nun sometimes, doesn't she? That one that's long with lots of frills and lots of cloth."

"Even when she was traveling long ago, the nun dress suited her."

"So that would look good on me, too."

Holo, the avatar of a wolf who would live for centuries, had the appearance of a young girl and stayed that way for years. And as Myuri grew, she and her mother had become two peas in a pod.

"Perhaps. Unlike you, Holo is calm and dignified."

"Hey!"

That is exactly what is different between them, he said to himself.

"I want something that's easy to move around in. And...I don't want to compete with Mother."

It seemed that girls were vain and prideful.

"Then we'll ask someone at the Debau Company to prepare a helper boy's outfit for you."

"What would happen if I were a prettier boy than you?"

He could only smile dryly, but Myuri got the shape of her face from her mother. Boy's clothes would surely suit her.

And it was much more difficult to spot a woman dressed as a man than the other way around.

"Well then, let's go," he said.

"Okay."

The town of Atiph sat on a hill on the south side of the river that flowed from east to west. The town square was at the highest point of the hill, and in typical southern style, all the town's important buildings, such as the church and town hall, encompassed it. Trade flourished here, so there were probably many southerners in the town's leadership.

According to what Col and Myuri heard at the stalls, the Debau Company's trading house was along the main street that extended from the square—fitting for its size. Perhaps someone who was familiar with the area would take the less populated back roads, but it was their first time here, so they followed the major avenues for the moment and decided to head for the square.

The money changers might be there, too.

"Whoa…," Myuri murmured in awe and peered up at the magnificent church standing before her.

The stone fortress at the port had also captivated her, but perhaps stone buildings themselves were new to her. The biggest buildings in Nyohhira were only three stories, and they were all made of wood. The church before her eyes was easily five stories tall, and the bell tower extended well above that. It was of a truly imposing scale.

"Hey, Brother…did they make this by stacking up each rock, one by one?"

"Yes. It takes considerable effort, but the harder they work, the more the strength of their faith shows. It is also a huge honor to quarry the heavy stone that will be used in the construction of a church. If you examine it closely, you can find the names of the people who donated carved into the stone."

"Wow…"

"Why don't you take a look? I need to replenish the change that a certain someone used up."

Myuri slowly lowered her gaze from the church to him, a wide grin on her face.

"Make sure you exchange a lot."

She was not shy about her wants.

"Just kidding. I would worry if you got lost, so I'll go with you."

"…"

Col looked at her as she stood next to him, and she truly seemed to be enjoying herself. He found himself smiling rather than sighing at her carefree attitude. Perhaps one could say he had no choice but to smile.

Then, they headed to the money changers, who sat on straw mats laid out around the statue of the Holy Mother in the center of the square. Not only travelers, but also a constant stream of townspeople were visiting them, perhaps to exchange money for shopping, and the money changers were frowning as they placed metals and coins on the scales. Among them, the pair found a money changer who had just gotten through his queue, and they called out to him.

"I'd like to exchange some money."

"All right, what do you need?"

There were no niceties—it was straight to the point. Col hurriedly pulled out his wallet and produced a single white silver piece.

"I'd like this in bronze *dip*, please."

"The coin of the sun, huh? That will be thirty bronze *dip* pieces."

"What?!"

Unwittingly, he yelled in surprise. The bronze *dip* was a piece of thin copper that was in circulation in this area, and one coin could buy about one piece of bread or one cup of ale. On the other hand, the silver coin engraved with the image of a sun was the strongest of its kind in this region, since it was also used for long-distance trade, and it was enough to feed a family of four for a week, with enough left over for a special treat on the Sabbath.

Before Col left, the owner of the bathhouse, Lawrence, told him about the exchange rates for all major coins, and he had said that this would gain him at least forty pieces—or if luck was on his side, then fifty pieces of bronze.

He thought perhaps they were being taken advantage of because they were travelers, but before he said anything, the money changer spread open the roll of parchment in his hand and recited the contents.

"An announcement from the city council: In view of the recent shortage of change, the city council has regulated the exchange rate between the silver coin of the sun and bronze *dip* as one to thirty."

He seemed used to the complaints of travelers.

"We appreciate a healthy economy, but because of that our supply of currency can't keep up. That's the case in other towns, too."

The money changer rolled up the parchment and placed it under the platform holding the scales.

"See, there's a big church in this town. *Everyone's* gone and put their change in that donation box of theirs."

Without looking, he pointed to the church with his thumb.

"On top of all that tax, you have to wonder what they're doing with all the coins sitting in that box...Oh, you're a traveling priest, huh?"

The money changer was not as apologetic as his words might suggest, and he grinned.

"So what will it be?"

"Ah…yes. Please."

"Thanks."

Col handed him the silver, and the money changer inspected the front and back, weighed it against raw silver on the scales, and finally handed him a bundle of bronze coins. There were exactly thirty. Perhaps the tout girl really was in trouble, and the stall owners did not want to give him change.

And Myuri's shopping for food became much more expensive.

"Young man, be sure to tell them they at least shouldn't let all that change sit in the box. The Church nowadays is all about money, money, money. We need the Kingdom of Winfiel to work hard."

Col could only smile dryly, and he put the coins away into his coin purse before leaving the money changers behind.

However, his heart began to race not when the money changer criticized the Church, but when he mentioned the Kingdom of Winfiel. Hearing the dissatisfaction of the townspeople directly felt like an endorsement of his mission.

How could the Church save the souls of the people after oppressing their livelihoods?

"Where to next, Brother?"

He responded with force.

"To the Debau Company."

He needed to meet up with Hyland quickly.

Stirred by a sense of purpose, he pulled a bewildered Myuri along and marched onto the main street.

Going south along the large road from the square, there appeared a block of similar-looking buildings. The first floor was always an unloading zone for cargo, and banners hung proudly from the second- and third-floor walls. These buildings belonged to the large commercial firms that held the reins of the town's economy. Among them, he found the familiar banner of the Debau Company.

"Oh…I've seen that design somewhere."

Myuri tilted her head.

"It was on the silver piece we just exchanged."

"Oh."

While the Debau Company was still a mercantile organization, it also issued the high-value silver *debau* on its own terms. The design on the face of the coin was that of a sun, and it was often called the "coin of the sun."

"That is a currency they could produce all thanks to your parents' efforts."

That was apparently the final uproar to liven up the journey of the merchant and the wolf avatar. Col truly thought they were amazing people, but this did not seem to click with Myuri herself.

The Debau Company building was a wide structure facing the street, and the first floor was an unloading zone. Merchants carrying packages that were larger than Col's body and wagons piled high with cargo were constantly coming and going.

The beggar-looking man crouching in a corner of the unloading area was likely watching to make sure no one was trying to steal things amid the commotion in exchange for charity. In addition to thieves, there were also stray cats and dogs that roamed around town, hoping to feed on pigs and chickens that ultimately strayed too far from their owners. He felt a slight pang of nostalgia, as it reminded him of when he was a wandering student, getting by with similar work.

"Hey, hey, you're in the way just standing there! If you want donations, try somewhere else!"

A man in the unloading area, steam rising from his bare upper body, shooed them away like he would a dog or cat.

"Ah, I need to pass on a message to the master of the house."

"Hah?"

"Please tell him my name is Tote Col. My plans to go to Lenos have changed to Atiph."

"Hmm?"

The man gazed at him suspiciously, but he shrugged his rough shoulders and disappeared inside.

And before long, he returned.

"Come in, he says. Who are you? A friend of that big shot?"

So it seemed that Hyland was already here.

He thanked the man, and they continued farther inside the unloading area.

Merchandise of all kinds had been stacked high, and after a step up was a reception desk, large enough to sleep on, with a blanket covering it. At the moment, that wide desk was also piled with coins and parchment, and there was a man buried among it all, writing. A large canvas hung on the wall behind him. Painted there was a larger-than-life angel, watching quietly over the merchants as they worked.

Such an impressive painting also stole Myuri's attention, but she did not seem moved or intimidated; instead, she tilted her head questioningly.

"I didn't know angels counted money, too. But why a sword? Is it a threat to keep them working?"

The angel held a sword in her right hand and the scales in her left. Col found himself smiling at her interpretation.

"The sword means justice, and the scales mean equality. But… it doesn't quite seem that way, does it?"

It seemed even more so because everyone was working as though something was driving them forward. It was just like being in the middle of a roaring hearth. He had thought he had a thing or two to say about diligence from working in the bath-house, but his job in Nyohhira was nowhere as trying as this. This was the speed at which the world moved.

He felt like scale deposits from the hot spring water had caked on him after living for ten years in the mountains, and they were slowly being chipped away.

"Ah, Sir Col, is it?"

The building was teeming with people no matter how far they continued in, and a well-dressed merchant called out to him. He wore clothes of a green cloth, dyed from what Col did not know, which gave him the air of a nobleman and signaled that he was the kind of merchant who only participated in major deals. His mustache was also groomed so that the ends bent sharply, like the horns of a bull. The man probably shaped them every morn-ing with egg whites.

"I received your message and came here. I am Tote Col."

"The chief in the main branch told me to take care of you. I am Stefan, head of this trading house."

They shook hands, and Stefan, who was certainly twenty-some years older than Col, turned his attention to Myuri, of course.

"And this young lady?"

"Hello. I am traveling with my brother due to certain circum-stances. I am Myuri."

She introduced herself clearly and with a smile as though this was expected. She acted so naturally that Stefan simply seemed to accept it. Such things did happen.

"We have prepared a room for you. Do you mind sharing?"

"Not at all. I hope we don't cause you too much trouble..."

"Nonsense. You treat us with the utmost respect, Sir Col."

The elegantly dressed Stefan was treating them with the highest level of etiquette, so Myuri's eyes widened in surprise. However, the Debau Company was deeply obliged to Lawrence and Holo, so it was just trickling down to Col.

"Is Heir Hyland already here?"

"Yes. Heir Hyland arrived two days ago by boat and has just returned from a meeting with the trade association—"

Stefan was cut off.

Just as he heard the sound of many footsteps coming from even farther in the unloading area from a connecting hallway, people stepped to the side, as though the sea were being parted. The person who appeared was of high status, accompanied by an attendant—his standing was immediately obvious because of the tailoring of his clothes and the air that surrounded him, which were clearly different from everyone else's. Or perhaps it was the shape of the face that drew even the gazes of men or the bright, eye-catching golden hair that displayed the blood of nobility. One could see why the legend of the golden sheep still existed to this day in the Kingdom of Winfiel.

It was Hyland himself.

"My, Heir Hyland."

Stefan interrupted himself and saluted, and Hyland stopped the man with the palm of his hand, as though commanding him to stand at ease.

Then, he turned to Col and smiled as if seeing an old friend.

Hurriedly, the boy copied Stefan and lowered his head.

"You seem to be in good spirits, Heir Hyland."

"And you have not changed, Sage Col."

Hyland was younger than he was and, with that unique, hoarse voice, deliberately called him "sage." The title of sage was one of power bestowed by the Church, and most of those who bore it were in universities. He could never imagine himself with such a title, but when Hyland said it, he almost believed it. Stefan and

Hyland's assistant seemed surprised, and he could not help but blush.

"You jest. The title of sage is an awesome one."

"Then why be so formal?"

Hyland spoke with a teasing grin.

"Col, I am no match for your scholarship, and we will be relying on your skills. However, it is not your job to curry favor with me."

He had said something similar when they debated at the bathhouse, but while a part of it was Hyland's honesty, another part of it was perhaps a plea.

When he spoke of currying favor as a job, the courteous Stefan appeared not to know what he was talking about, to an unnatural extent.

"All right. I have always spoken like this, however."

"Very well." Hyland smiled a boyish, innocent smile, then continued with a wry one. "And who is this girl? Why is she here?"

"*Hiss!*"

Myuri poked her head out from behind Col, baring her teeth at Hyland.

"Ha-ha, lively as always. Mr. Stefan, we had sugar and blueberry candies, yes? I want to give her some."

Stefan had been watching them blankly, but as the master merchant that he was, he immediately nodded politely.

"Then later for supper," Hyland said, then walked off briskly.

His attendant followed after him, and Col felt as though the heavy air had suddenly lightened.

That must be the noble presence.

"Myuri, do not be so rude."

Myuri was glaring at Hyland as he exited the building, and when Col spoke, she puffed her cheeks and looked away.

"But I'll take the candy."

She grumbled, even more dissatisfied, and Col nudged her in the head, sighing in exasperation.

Their room was on the third floor. It was typically meant for merchants who were visiting the company. There was only one bed, so the boy who brought them there offered to prepare another one, but they could not ask so much. In addition, Myuri was not a bad sleeper, so it did not bother Col terribly. Of course, he also did not see her as a member of the opposite sex.

Therefore, instead of a bed, they asked for a disguise for Myuri.

"Hey, Brother?"

As he reached into his bag and retrieved several worn pens and a heavily annotated copy of the scripture, Myuri called out to him.

"Where are we right now? This is a world map, right?"

Myuri was standing in front of a large diagram hanging on the wall.

The map had been drawn on a single piece of leather, and it was big enough to wrap around Myuri. It was not the parchment of a sheep but probably of one entire young cow.

"We're around here."

The southern metropolis, where the pope resided, was in the middle of the map. Using that as a guideline, Atiph would be quite far in the upper left corner.

"Where's Nyohhira?"

"Up the river from Atiph here."

He pointed to the edge of the map, under the beard of a decorative sun with a human face.

"Ah-ha-ha. It's the edge of the world."

"And yet, people there are leading lives just as active."

"You traveled a long time ago too, right, Brother? Where was that?"

"Let's see...," he answered honestly, but Myuri's curiosity was endless. A knock at the door interrupted them, so he happily broke off.

"Myuri, stop staring at the map and come change."

What arrived were the set of boy's clothes and the sugar and blueberry candies that Hyland mentioned to Stefan.

"Oh, wow!"

Of course, it was not the boy's clothes that excited her. Her ears and tail popped out so forcefully he could almost hear it, and when she flew forward, he quickly spun her around.

"You may eat after you change."

There was a fair difference in their heights, so once he held the tray of candies above his head, Myuri could not reach them. She looked at him sadly, but when he shook his head, her expression suddenly became quite cross. With that rapid change in her visage, she snatched the clothes up.

"Sheesh, what a pain..."

Grumbling, she went to change, and as she carelessly shucked off her clothes, he of course left the room.

"What? But you always see me in the bath!"

Myuri sounded puzzled, but that was not the problem. He leaned against the door and sighed.

Her mother, Holo, almost never hesitated to show skin, which was of course expected from the embodiment of a wolf.

And so it would be shameful if he protested too much and appeared to have wicked feelings, but upon further consideration, no, she should be a virtuous maiden.

However, when he saw Myuri naked without the clouding steam

of Nyohhira, it was a little different than he imagined. At some point, the hard angles on her thin and rather muscular-looking body had begun to disappear. Though she was not quite fully matured, he could probably predict what was to come.

While he was joyful at the thought of how she was properly growing up, he also felt a bit sad for some reason.

"My bashful brother, I'm changed!"

As he waited, absentmindedly eating candy, he heard her rude call from the other side of the door.

When he opened the door and entered the room, a pretty young boy was standing there.

"Eh-heh-heh. What do you think?"

"...I'm shocked. Appearances really are important."

While the fine make of the clothes certainly had something to do with it, the starched trousers and slim-fitted sleeves, the spotless, thin vest, and the long sash wrapping around her waist made her into the very image of a young boy who took orders beside a great merchant.

"But what should I do about my hair? I guess I can just tie it up like yours, huh?"

Though Col was growing his out because it was too much of a bother to cut it, Myuri's hair was much longer.

"It may be best to braid it nicely."

"Okay."

She brought the chair from under the desk over to where Col was, then reached out and snatched the tray of candy from him. After that, Myuri sat in the chair, her back facing him.

"Mm."

It was as though she was commanding him to braid her hair. He did not have the energy to be angry.

He retrieved a comb from Myuri's things and began running

it through her hair while she happily stuffed her face with candy. The strands had a strange texture—soft and slightly cool to the touch. There was quite a lot of it, so he set about making two braids and then twisting them together.

"Still…This is all such a pain."

"What, do you mean the effort required in taking care of you?"

"Nuh-uh!" Myuri said, leaning backward over the chair to look at him upside down. "I mean how I have to hide my ears and tail and how I have to hide that I'm a girl."

"That's how the world is. Come now, sit up straight."

He poked her head, and she obediently fixed her posture. It had been a while since he braided her hair, and it was surprisingly entertaining. She used to always pester him to braid her hair. As he recalled how she had eventually stopped doing that, she spoke up again.

"Hey, Brother?"

"What is it?"

He finished one braid and took hold of the next section of hair. He combed through it again, but Myuri did not continue.

"Is something wrong?" he asked again, and the hand she had been eating candy with stopped moving. She spoke in a tone of voice he could not read.

"Is there a place on that map where I don't have to hide my ears and tail?"

His hands stopped automatically. He looked up, and before the sitting Myuri was the massive world map. Even a large town like Atiph only occupied one corner of the map, and it was doubtful if Nyohhira was even on it. The world was so big and filled with endless possibilities.

And then, he realized it.

Perhaps that was the very reason Myuri wanted to leave Nyohhira.

"That's…"

But his words caught in his throat.

Myuri was almost never let out of her room in the bathhouse until she was old enough to know what was going on. When she was, everything but her face was completely wrapped in cloth. Her parents explained to those around her that she was weak and could not handle the steam from the baths, but it was, of course, to hide her ears and tail.

By the time she understood what was what, her mother, Holo, told her about her heritage, the concept of demonic possession, and that if they were found out, they could no longer stay in Nyohhira.

He remembered it like it was yesterday, the day she learned the truth and how she came crying to him with her questions.

"Will no one want to be my friend anymore?"

As someone who dreamed of being a priest, it was clear how he should answer: When you are in pain, when you are sad, when you feel lonely, if you lift your eyes to the sky, you will see your own eternal companion. However, at that time, what he said was something else.

"At the very least, no matter what happens to me, I will always be your friend."

That day, Myuri learned that the world was a dark, cold place and desperately searched for something to rely on. He sensed that, in order for his words to reach her heart just then, he needed conviction sturdier than any stone. His gut had told him he needed to tell her he believed in her—words that he could speak with full confidence. He could not even speak for her father, Lawrence, much less for a god who had yet to look his way. As long as he was speaking only for himself, it was a solid promise.

Then, Myuri had smiled. *"I'm glad,"* she said, smiling.

Ever since then, Myuri had accepted her fate, learned how to hide her ears and tail, and lived in Nyohhira as a (questionably) regular girl. He thought she had gotten over it a long time ago, but perhaps it was not so easy.

"That's…"

His hands that had been braiding her hair were still stopped.

He had a sense that lies and consolation would convey themselves to her through his hands.

More than anything, it would be rude to her to underestimate her as someone who could be easily tricked.

"That might be difficult."

The world was supported by the Church, as the pope's throne was in the center of the map. Even in places that respected local legends, it was still a gamble as to whether or not nonhumans would be accepted.

"Myuri, but—"

"It's okay," Myuri said, bending back and looking at him again. "Like Mother has Father, I have you. Right?"

Her smile was more mature than it used to be. She was purposely twisting her body in a strange way, and he realized it was her way of being considerate by hiding her seriousness.

"…Right. I'm surprised how well you remember, considering you never listen to what I say."

Like Col himself and Lawrence, there would always be people who understood. She would be fine as long as she found companions like that.

Myuri closed her eyes and furrowed her brows, baring her teeth at him. Leaning back, she seemed about to fall, and he hurriedly caught her, but apparently she had trusted him to do just that.

Her eyes still closed, Myuri had a relatively calm expression on her face.

"Then it's all right. We're always together."

She opened her eyes, smiling shyly, and sat up straight.

"Come now, Brother, hurry up and braid my hair. I want to see the attractions in town."

"Attractions? We did not come here for fun, you know," Col scolded her.

Though her thin shoulders shook in laughter, from behind, Myuri seemed a little lonely. Unlike her mother, Holo, she had not lived for hundreds of years. Though she could catch the biggest of adults off guard in an argument, she was still very much the young girl that she appeared to be. From here on, she would experience many troubles and hardships. He could not protect her from them all, but he wanted to do what he could.

He wove his feelings neatly into Myuri's hair.

Neither of them could say a word.

They spent the time in silence.

Once Myuri was done preparing, they went to see Stefan and ask about *Our Book of God*, but it was just as crowded in front of the office as it had been in the unloading area.

"Brother, what is this?"

A wide variety of individuals stood in front of Stefan's office in the innermost part of the first floor, from the well-dressed to those clothed not so nicely, and they all wore grave expressions on their faces. Many were accompanied by attendants, and with the chore boys of the Debau Company darting among them taking orders, it was much more congested than necessary.

From what Col could hear from the chatter, it sounded like they had come to make various requests.

"The seasons are about to change, so perhaps everyone is here for their expenses."

There were people from nearby villages who had come to borrow money to replenish the stock used up during the winter and others from craftsmen associations who wanted to have their purchasing allowance increased. There were also merchants who had traveled a long distance from faraway lands on trading vessels and came offering souvenirs.

Winter had long finished by this time of year in the south, and time was now moving again. The northern towns and villages, where ports and roads would freeze over during the winter, needed to fill their emptied storehouses, too, and prepare for festivals while getting ready to plant seeds for spring.

The seasons changed for everybody, but that did not mean goods were distributed evenly.

And so people gathered at large companies like this in the hopes of gaining even a slight advantage.

"Is everyone here to see him? Such an important person came out to meet you, Brother."

"Have you reconsidered your opinion of him?"

"Yeah. I was just thinking how Mother and Father helped out in such an amazing place."

Myuri smiled at him, and he smiled in return.

Several moments later, she said happily, "Don't be so pouty, Brother."

In between the exchanges, Col had caught hold of a boy and explained their business. Typically they would wait their turn, but no matter how he figured, nobody was going in order. A group of men, clearly from another country—with cloth wrapped around their heads, gold decorating their necks, and skin darkened from the sun—had just come from the back when they were called into the office.

Was it money? Authority? Importance?

God would not punish Col if he used Hyland's influence, as well as Lawrence and Holo's connections.

The helper boy wove through the crowd and entered the office, and he returned before long.

"Everyone came rather suddenly, so they will be processing the large volume of requests now."

He could not blame them. It was due to all this commotion.

"Then we shall gather people and tools." The priest-in-training declared his intentions before continuing on. "Shall we handle the payments?"

"We will take care of all your expenses, Sir Col."

"You have my thanks," Col replied, then signaled to Myuri with his eyes and left the packed building.

It was just as clamorous outside, but without a roof, the supply of air seemed infinite.

"Wow, Brother, did you hear that?"

Once outside, that was the first thing Myuri said.

"They said they'll foot the bill. So you don't need to worry about your savings."

"We are not going shopping for food."

"Aw, why?"

"Footing the bill is a sign of respect. We should act in a way that is deserving of that respect. If we constantly demand payment for street food, what do you expect they'll think of us?"

"Um…That we're hungry…"

"…"

He sensed something like a headache coming on and simply walked forward for the moment.

"Moderation is not simply cutting down on amounts. It is a moral duty to control yourself so that you are not steered by your whims—what you want to eat, drink, or buy," he said. He also suddenly hit upon the difference between moderation and stinginess. "And so being a miser is not regulating yourself, but being especially absorbed in gaining any sort of thing—in this case, coin. Do you understand?"

He heard once that sermons were meant for the enlightenment of oneself as well as the people, but this was the first time he saw how firsthand.

"Kind of, I think…"

Myuri caught up to his side and seemed even more displeased.

"So you can't gain anything from moderation, right? So why do it?"

"Ah."

This was not one of the questions she asked knowing it would catch him off-balance. He knew immediately when she was simply expressing doubt. Yet her very straightforward query had incredible depth to it.

Why? For what reason?

Legitimate-sounding responses reached the tip of his tongue, but they all felt wrong.

As he walked deep in thought, a wagon nearly ran him over. The one who grabbed his sleeve and used all her weight to pull him back was none other than Myuri.

"Brother, you dummy!"

"I'm sorry."

However, he was not apologizing about the cart. He was sorry for his inability to answer her simple question.

The importance of moderation was, of course, promoted in the scripture, as well as taught as a virtue, but many things that were considered good were not written there. When he considered why temperance was right, he got the sense that a reason did not exist.

If it did, then there was only one.

"Because, perhaps, it just seems like it's the right thing to do."

Myuri regarded him with a dubious expression.

"I'm sure some people cannot stand it, but even they most likely understand the goodness of moderation itself."

"…"

He asked himself again, ignoring Myuri as her dubious expression shifted to a worried one.

Perhaps it was wrong to simply pursue an idea on the basis that it was a given.

He had a feeling there was an ancient philosopher who had proclaimed that goodness was defined as what was natural.

"However, if that were the case, what would become of vowing abstinence…?"

A marriage was cause for celebration, but priests encouraged suppression of the natural desire that came with it.

Was being free of want natural?

Who would agree that abstinence was natural?

"Hmm…"

When one questions all that they have accepted as normal, they may find once unthinkable things lying in wait on the path ahead of them. As he stood in the street, pondering, someone pulled on his sleeve.

There was Myuri, looking ready to cry.

"Brother…I won't be so selfish anymore, so please forgive me…"

"What?" he replied, and she frantically clung to him. He did not know what she had been saying to him, but she seemed to think the way he had stopped and stood still was a reaction to her desire to shop for food. He looked down at Myuri holding him, and a thought flickered across his mind.

Maybe next time she would grab his hand.

"Oh, I was just thinking too much," he said and placed his hand on Myuri's head, ruffling her hair to calm her down. But due to her unexpected question, his mind ran in circles like a bird that could not find a tree to land on.

Despite his restless, vague discomfort, he was a bit excited to see where the bird would go.

The town was divided into districts with the square in the center, so anyone who became lost could simply find the bell tower that was visible from anywhere and head to the plaza. The layout was impressively logical.

Col walked, Myuri was in tow and no longer appealing for food, and they made their way toward the craftsmen's district. Appropriate for the port town that Atiph was, there were a great many woodworking studios. And under the eaves of a workshop that cut and whittled, thick black tree resin was being brushed onto lumber. Col thought that Myuri, who had hidden in a barrel meant for that resin, would frown at the familiar smell, but she watched the work intensely.

"So that's how they use it."

"They apparently use it for waterproofing and to protect against mold. When trading vessels go to distant lands, or ships go off to war, they use it for packaging meat so it doesn't go bad."

"Huh. It has a smoky scent, so maybe it would taste good."

I see, it depends on your perspective, he thought.

They continued farther down before arriving at an area that worked with furs. In the open-air first-floor workshops, there were artisans working on each stage of tanning the hides and crafting leather cord.

There was a neat line of warm-looking ermine furs, and he wondered which nobles would buy them.

As they continued, they arrived at a shop that had a giant cow hide hanging on the wall facing the street, which the owner must have been using in place of a sign.

"Is that what they used for the map?"

Myuri sniffed the hide, and a man fiddling with the handle of a razor in the workshop noticed them.

"Do you need somethin'?"

Myuri whispered to Col, "We could probably sell his fur," and he had to suppress his smile. The fellow was indeed a hairy craftsman, big both sideways and lengthways, a complete bear of a man.

"You don't often see a young priest and an errand boy from the Debau Company together. Are you looking for something to write on?"

Col jabbed the mischievous Myuri in the head and cleared his throat before speaking.

"I need scrap paper, ink, parchment, and talc."

He would grate the talc and then rub it into the uneven parchment in order to flatten it.

"All right, leave it to me!…is what I want to say, but we just got a large order for parchment yesterday, so we're in the middle of making more now."

The crafts-bear shrugged his shoulders, reached out to the parchment on the worktable, and waved it.

"I need to make five sheets out of this. Your average craftsman can get about three, though."

He casually boasted about his skill, but five sheets was rather impressive. Parchment was made from the hide of animals, so unlike paper made from old rags, how thinly it could be cut depended on the maker's skill.

"Are other workshops also busy with similar orders?" Col asked, and the crafts-bear stared at him blankly before bursting out into laughter.

"You must be from a big city. The only ones that deal in parchment and stationery around here are our workshop and our group. This ain't the kind of town with thousands of notaries constantly ordering parchment."

"I see…"

If so, then what happened?

He groaned, and the crafts-bear seemed to have suddenly realized something.

"Wait, now that you mention it, that order from yesterday was supposed to be delivered to the Debau Company."

"What?"

"Yeah, that's right. Now I remember. A whole troupe of nicely dressed folk came and asked for all the paper we had…I was so happy we sold out of parchment that I forgot."

At the news that a well-dressed group had asked for all the paper they had to be delivered to the Debau Company, Col could only think of one possibility.

As it crossed his mind, a thin old man with a white beard, the exact opposite of the bearlike craftsman, appeared from inside the shop.

"Oh, customers, I see."

"Oh, Old Boss, who was it that made that big order yesterday?"

"Ah? Your brain can only ever think about how fine you can slice leather, eh? You'll never be able to do business like that. The request was from a noble from the Kingdom of Winfiel."

So it was Hyland.

"Really? What's an island noble doing here?"

"Geez…Haven't I told you to go show up at association meetings? Their kingdom and the Church are in a dispute over tithes, remember? The kingdom thinks those taxes are absurd, and that nobleman is their spokesman. He's come to convince Atiph's Church that they should work together. And it appears he wants to make nice with the townspeople first, so he's having meetings with every association. That's where I've been all morning."

"Oh. Huh..."

The crafts-bear was clearly not interested, as he was glancing down at his razor. Watching them, Col empathized more with the old bearded man.

"*Huh?* Is that all you have to say? Idiot. If that nobleman succeeds, we won't have to pay taxes to the Church anymore."

"Oh, that'd be great. They always say the pope's feasts are extravagant. It would be nice if we didn't have to pay for their luxuries."

It was a coarse way of saying it, but what the crafts-bear said was likely exactly how the townspeople felt.

"But what does that have to do with the order?"

As he stroked the blade of the razor, the old bearded man thumped him on the head without hesitation. There was a solid *thud*.

Then, the old man turned to face them, squinting as if they were shining bright.

"If you've brought along a boy from the Debau Company, does that mean you've come to help that nobleman?"

"Ah, yes."

"My, I've known about the kingdom for a long time, but today I learned so much at the meeting. Especially that Heir Hyland is such a wonderful person. He dreams up ideas I could never imagine," the old man said. He shook Col's hand and took the opportunity to grasp Myuri's hand as well, bowing deeply.

"Us lowly people honestly never thought either side, whether the Church or the kingdom, had anything to do with us. But I never imagined that the scripture would be translated into the common language nor that we would be asked to look directly upon the words of God! Oh, what a wonderful thing this is."

As the old man spoke, he began to choke up.

"Pardon me...At any rate, though we've had enough of the

pope and the Church's luxury and lack of restraint, we're not in a place to fight back. This is a port town. Only God knows if there will be an accident at sea. If we were ordered to cease all religious activities, the root of life in this town would wither away. Ordinary courage is not enough to send ships into the pitch-black sea to be ravaged by the cold winds of winter. And accidents never stop. If you live in this town, you will most certainly have someone who works with the sea in your family."

After negotiations with the cathedra in Lenos failed, there was more than enough reason to switch over to Atiph instead. The locals bestowed upon ships the name of saints and carved images of the Holy Mother or icons of angels onto the bows for protection on their voyages. Anyone who saw the haul of cod and herring caught in the port could understand they had a great number of fishermen. In addition, this was not like the warm, mild seaside towns in the southlands. Beyond this town was a frigid, gray sea, where there was no chance of survival for people who fell off a boat.

"It is truly an honor for us to assist directly. As you can see, I'm already so old, and this bear can only be relied upon for his skills."

Apparently, everyone looked at the craftsman and saw a bear. Myuri lowered her head, trying to suppress her laugh.

"We've got scribe friends that we've already talked to, so leave the copies to us. As soon as you make progress on your translation, we'll make more and more of them, and we'll let everyone know how ridiculous the Church is!"

This old man and the townspeople had no reason to doubt the protection of God. They were simply dissatisfied with the corrupt practices of the Church's inner circle, who were God's representative on earth.

Col once again recognized that what the Kingdom of Winfiel was doing was not barbaric, but necessary.

The world he believed in lay just beyond this.

God's true teachings were what Hyland was aiming for.

"Let us work hard together," he said, gripping the old man's hand in return.

"Myuri, have you now come to understand how amazing Heir Hyland is?"

He posed his question to Myuri on their way back from the workshop, and she nodded, albeit reluctantly.

For the rest of the day, they walked around town for a little bit. They spent some time looking at the city walls under construction and the gray sea from a hill before returning to the trading house.

That night, they were invited to a dinner that Stefan presided over with Hyland as the guest of honor, and they discussed things that were neither good nor bad. However, as Col watched the goings-on at the supper, he sensed something other than flattery in Stefan's courteousness toward Hyland.

"Perhaps. Speaking to the townspeople, everyone seemed surprised that I was staying in the Debau Company trading house. Sir Stefan, the master of the house, apparently shares a hometown with the pope, you see, and has a deep connection through sending them goods. It's unbelievable that he would accommodate one who would oppose the Church such as myself. Sir Stefan has reluctantly let me stay because management told him to. Merchants like him are more concerned about the profits before them than righteousness. Even in the absence of tithes, if the Church were to lose its funds, then the number of business transactions would decrease accordingly, and that is as far as his thoughts take him."

After supper, Hyland called the pair to his room. Col was more concerned during supper about keeping a smile on his face, so he did not clearly remember what he ate. Myuri had brazenly stuffed herself with food, and at first was reluctant to go, saying she could not move, but when she learned there would be candy, she came along shamelessly.

"So the Debau Company is not a monolith, after all," said Col.

"Such a big company is the same as a country. It would be impossible to unite them in consensus, to say nothing of their status as merchants. They go round and round more than weather vanes on the roof."

Lawrence, whom he always greatly respected, was a former merchant, so Col simply let it go with a smile. "However, when I went to the craftsmen's workshop to arrange for the paper, I listened to their story and was convinced. The ceasing of all religious activities really is wrong."

"I was surprised, too, talking to all the associations in town, since their responses were so much different from those in Lenos. It was as though I'd become a savior."

Hyland spoke with a coarse voice and a smile, bringing wine to his lips.

"Though this was originally pagan land, this is a town founded when those from the south came by boat and settled here. They fear the world outside their walls. They believe there are monsters hidden in the depths of the sea and that there is nothing that humanity can do about it. There is a stronger appreciation for God here compared to other places. That being said…"

Hyland affectionately crinkled his eyes, resting his chin in his hand and setting his arm on the armrest of the chair as he watched Myuri. She showed no interest in the teachings of God as she cradled a tray of dried sugared apples and munched on them. The plethora of sugared fruits was available because of the many rich people who needed to divert themselves from the boredom on long sea journeys.

"Most people act for material gain. They cannot stand having to pay taxes." Hyland playfully eyed Myuri, who had tagged along when she heard there would be candy. "You saw the city walls under construction, yes? And the impressive paved road from the port."

"It's a wonderful town."

"To be more precise, it is currently struggling to become a wonderful town. They are suffocating under the tax that has been levied on them. For all the activity it sees, this town is not very rich."

There was likely information from the Debau Company about that.

"In addition, the cathedra in this town has a short history and low standing within the Church. More importantly, the archbishop here has never been placed in the church of a town with a good economy."

The smiles of those in high ranks were sometimes terribly cold-blooded.

"He rises and thinks that all the money that comes through the Church is for himself. And yet, the townspeople all say that he is a hard worker."

Greedy yet fervent in his work for the Church—the two did not connect in Col's head.

Hyland looked at him and chuckled.

"Col, you should look beyond the world of books, too."

"…I'm sorry."

"What I mean is that a longsword has its advantages, but you cannot use it like short sword."

Hyland poured more wine into the cup and spoke.

"I'm sure he cannot tell the difference between the church and his home. So though he is wholly committed to his sacred work for himself, on the other hand, he considers the church his own and lives so deep in selfishness. It's likely that he does not even see it as selfishness. But from the outside, it's clear. They say the most affluent woman in this town is the archbishop's wife, after all."

"That's…"

"Of course, she's not his official wife, but everyone knows it. That being said…"

Hyland shrugged.

"There is no honor in attacks against me as an illegitimate child."

It was not uncommon for nobles and royalty to reach out to women who were not their wives, and the similar activities of priests who vowed to stay single were an open secret.

That was how it was.

"However, the archbishop here has not quite managed to do it successfully. My father was forced to marry the pope's niece or something like that, but the people saw true love between him and my mother. And even from my perspective, he is quite charming."

Hyland's words hinted at something, but Col understood what he wanted to say.

"On the other hand, because the archbishop is so dedicated to his work, he often becomes overbearing. It is necessary that he be used to wielding power, but it seems he does not understand. He is strict with the sins of capriciousness and adultery, but the people wonder what right he has to say such things considering his own actions. When he preaches of moderation, one can only listen with a smile."

The bear of a craftsman had also said that the suppers at the church were always extravagant.

"And yet they recognize the passion for his work when he cries for someone's passing, cries in the joy of a wedding, cries at birth. That is why the people wish to do something about these twisted feelings they have for the Church. The clergy are worryingly two-faced: They live in licentiousness with the money gained from the heavy taxes on the people, yet they are reliable when it comes to their holy work."

"It is not that the people don't want to respect them."

"Or rather, to borrow the words of God, they want to love them. Well, perhaps 'esteem' might be better." Hyland smiled.

Once the water of faith flowed properly, the world would become clearer.

"That is why the *Our Book of God* plan is so well received among the people. Some are already pestering me to show them any part that has been finished."

"When I went to the workshop to prepare paper and ink, the boss there was cheering me on."

Hyland smiled and gave a signal to his chamberlain waiting in the corner of the room. Then, a young man around the same age as Col, with the airs of a civil servant about him, handed him a bundle of parchments.

"My father agreed with this plan from very early on and is in the process of gathering all the idle priests throughout the country. For the most part, in the name of lecturing on God's teachings. They cannot eat if they do not work, and they have a favorable view of my father, so it is going well, it seems. However, those living in their ivory towers have some trouble when it comes to the vernacular. They eagerly want to hear the opinions of opposing scholars."

He did not say "sage," but it still made Col uncomfortable to hear "scholar."

As though he had noticed his feelings, Hyland chuckled.

"Col. I, too, recognize humility as a virtue, but you will find that how others around you see you very much depends on who speaks up first."

He was telling him to be proud of himself.

"I will devote myself to it."

Hyland smiled in relief.

"The translation is going well, and parts from earlier are written on this parchment, but I need you to move it along, too. Once I send it home, it will be a great help to them."

It was awe-inspiring, but this was what it meant to face a grand prospect. Col braced himself and took the parchment. Translating the scripture into the common language would educate the people, and it might be fair to call it one of the battles for correcting the ridiculousness of the Church. When he thought about how this work would be his weapon, his shield, it felt much heavier.

"I understand," he replied with strength, and Hyland smiled, satisfied.

"And I expect you to work hard for all the candy the young lady has eaten."

With a kind gaze, Hyland watched Myuri lick the sugar off her fingers over an empty tray. As they all watched her while her finger was in her mouth, even she seemed a bit uncomfortable.

"The only ones who have ever done such a thing in my presence are clowns protected by privilege and their daughters."

"I sincerely apologize…Myuri!"

Col scolded Myuri, and she ducked with a defiant look.

"No, that's all right. We are sticking our necks into a fight against authority. Authority makes people blind and takes away their ability to think. Not to mention their courage to call out oddities when they see them. I do not lie when I say I expect great things from you. So...can you read?"

Myuri stared back blankly at Hyland's question.

"Letters. Not the Church's script."

"Ah yes, a little," Col answered for her, and Hyland rejoiced.

"I see. Then, I'm sure this is quite boring for young ladies like you, but I want you to look over the scripture. I'm sure you may perceive some truths that are much beyond us."

Myuri wore an expression of slight pride, but Hyland was likely overestimating her.

"Heir Hyland, you say that, but—" Col began to give advice.

"It's not flattery. I feel something about her. The mistress of the bathhouse I stayed in was the same...Perhaps she's from some sort of distinguished house?"

He was startled when he heard Hyland's speculation. If Holo and Myuri's bloodline were to be called a distinguished house, then it would quite literally be something beyond human comprehension. Including supernatural beings in the establishing tales of a family line was done by only the highest of the many high-status royal families in the world.

"See, Brother? People that know, know."

However, Myuri had puffed out her chest, unaware of his worry. There was no hint of humility.

"Ha-ha-ha. This young lady here understands how the world works."

Had her tail been out, it would have been swishing right about then.

"Don't take it at face value," he warned her, but she did not show any sign of responding.

"Well, I won't investigate. It is in the scripture, too."

Hidden things would someday be let loose.

He could not tell if it was a good thing at this point in time.

"And I have confidence in you."

He heard Hyland as someone who stood above others, taming his vassals. It was not that he held any contempt for Hyland himself, as he was a noble, but if he did not warn himself that he and Myuri were different, they would be swallowed whole. Hyland was an enchanting person, and it would be wonderful if he could become a priest with his own cathedra under the man's dominion.

However, he wanted to cooperate as much as possible without self-interest. At stake was something far greater than the profits of any individual.

"To the first step of righting the world."

Hyland cheered and raised high a glass of wine.

CHAPTER THREE

That night, after receiving the parchment with the translation of the scripture, Col barely slept. He was glued to the desk, absorbed in reading it and referencing the original as he went on. He was inundated with intellectual stimuli, constantly surprised by some of the interpretations and wordings.

He vaguely remembered Myuri becoming upset about being unable to sleep because of the bright candle, but she had gone silent at some point.

Then, he suddenly realized he could hear a wagon passing outside. He felt like he had been reading the translation until that very moment, but apparently he had fallen asleep, and a blanket was draped over his shoulders. He looked at the bed where Myuri was curled up sleeping. She somehow seemed exasperated.

Having fallen asleep in the same position in the cold, his body felt like a dried branch. He slowly loosened up, and after deciding to take a quick snooze, he crawled into bed. His tension eased when he felt the warmth under the covers from Myuri's body heat, and he instantly fell asleep.

When he next awoke, he bolted upright in a sudden wave of regret and fear.

"The lunch preparations!"

The sun was already high in the sky, and from the color of the light, he could immediately tell that breakfast had already finished at the bathhouse and it was time to get ready for lunch. He instantly felt a cold sweat and the need to apologize to Lawrence, who was likely working hard making arrangements. Lamenting how he had broken his streak of never waking up late over these past few years, he got out of bed, and that was when he realized—

"…Good morning?" Myuri, sitting at the desk and combing her hair, raised a perplexed greeting.

"Oh…Right, this isn't the bathhouse…"

He could hear the sounds of a bustling town from beyond the open window.

There was a faint scent of salt.

"You really like to work, Brother."

Myuri smiled, astonished.

"Oh, and while you were being Mr. Sleepyhead and snoozing your time away, a package came."

Myuri was typically the one being scolded for sleeping in, so she was enjoying her chance to nip at him. It was perhaps too much to expect her to wake him up. There was no doubt that she gloated upon rising and finding him still asleep.

He could not forget to inspect his face and clothes for pranks.

Then, he looked at the package, and his sleepiness immediately evaporated.

"Myuri, move."

"Wha—?"

He picked up the parcel that had been laid next to the door and placed it with a *thud* onto the desk. Myuri, shooed away, reluctantly sat down on the bed.

"This is enough to…"

Inside, there were many sheets of paper made from rags and

118

as much parchment made from sheep as he could carry. The ink was practically overflowing, and there were enough quill pens to carry him into the air.

"Are you going to use all that by yourself, Brother?"

Myuri looked astonished, sitting cross-legged on the bed and tying her hair back.

"No, there are scribes who should be working with us…Myuri, did anyone come to visit?"

"Hmm, oh, someone came and asked if you were here, but when I told them you were sleeping, they were all, 'okay, we'll be waiting.'"

"That's them!" he said and was about to exit the room in one big stride when Myuri called out to him.

"Ah, hey, Brother! What about breakfast?!"

"As you like!" he said and exited the room.

The day's work at the Debau Company had started long ago, and it was still just as crowded as it was the day before. After Col described things to a passing errand boy, the boy brought him to a corner of the unloading area where several men sat idle. When they noticed him, they heaved themselves up as though with great effort. They all had stooped shoulders and bandages wrapped around their right hands. They each carried a worn-out bag on their shoulders, and their clothes were stained as though they had been dragged through mud and water. Their hands and faces were just as mottled as their clothes were.

To someone who did not know who they were, they seemed nothing but poor travelers or farmers escaping a heavy tax on their village. However, just as mercenaries proud of their demonic strength would be covered in the blood of their victims, excellent scribes were covered in ink.

Though every other part of these men seemed impoverished, their eyes shone brightly.

119

"We hope we may be of some use in sharing the correct teachings of God."

"Of course. Thank you so much for coming."

Col shook hands with all three of them and thanked them for reaching Atiph.

"Are you not busy around this time of year, though?"

"Ha-ha-ha. I suppose. My notary master ordered me to come, however."

"I am from the tax collector association in the port."

"I've come from the city council library."

Those who could read and write were treasured, and those who could copy books were priceless. That work was more difficult than anyone could imagine, and it was taught as a way of penance in monasteries. It was a task not many people would offer to carry out, and those who would do so with perseverance and without complaint were few indeed.

Hyland must have gone through those papermakers to gather these scribes, so they were probably quite skilled. The places they had been pulled away from were in all likelihood incredibly busy.

"Still, by helping Heir Hyland, and by extension the Kingdom of Winfiel, our masters supposes that the benefits will outweigh our missing services. The tithes are applied to many things, after all. It would not be odd for one or two craftsmen like myself to earn their fortunes should taxes vanish."

"And it seems other large craftsmen associations are having their subordinates spread Heir Hyland's ideas and sending people out to collect funds in front of the Church when the time calls for it. However, by the nature of our work, we do not have very many potential masters to work for. If we didn't contribute at all and then the tithes were actually repealed, we would lose our place in town."

"In addition, everyone is simply interested in what is written in the scriptures. They are not satisfied by the Church's excuses and wonder what God is really saying."

He could clearly tell from their responses that Hyland's plan was going well.

He felt an indescribable excitement when he thought how the world might change.

"According to Heir Hyland, you are a very knowledgeable theologian."

"Please, teach us."

"Oh...ah...oh no, far from it. I am honored."

It seemed Hyland was praising him everywhere, but it was also possibly a bluff to encourage the people. Hyland was not a noble with only a good personality to his name.

"Well, well, this is the first time I've met a priest who has adopted the virtue of humility."

"Indeed, how inspiring."

Col had a feeling that this was also part of Hyland's strategy, and he could do nothing but smile dryly as he stood before the awestruck scribes.

Then, securing a workspace for them was another trouble. The Debau Company trading house appeared to have been simply thrown together by connecting a number of different buildings with corridors, and it was so complicated and big, they would be lost without a map.

Even still, every room was full of people, and they ended up using the room Col and Myuri were borrowing.

"Myuri, hold this."

They pushed the bed and furniture all up against the wall and brought in desks from other rooms.

The room suddenly transformed into a copy room of a workshop or a church, and only Myuri sat on the bed, hugging her knees.

"So what is it we will be copying?"

"Here it is. Please divide the work among yourselves."

"I hope all the spelling has been corrected. I cannot read, you see."

It was not unusual for a scribe to be illiterate. Letters were like pictures, and those who could copy them could do the work. Rather, this was preferred, since they could more faithfully re-create the original. The problem was that any mistakes would also be perfectly copied.

"I have for everything I was able to understand..."

If the scribe did not know how to read, then he would not know what parts had already been corrected. That being said, it would not be good to scribble notes directly on the parchment where the translation was. As Col wondered about how to approach the issue, the man produced a pincushion from his bag and said, "Please rest assured. Insert the pins onto the words that have spelling mistakes, and then I will refer to them and fix the spelling."

"Excellent."

He admired the craftsman's rational wisdom. He quickly began placing pins into the man's allotted parchment.

The other two men were wrapping cloth around their wrists and preparing small armrests that they seemed to typically use while they worked. They truly called to mind warriors preparing to go into battle, which was promising. Before long, their setup for work was completed.

"Then, let us stir life into the Church."

One of the craftsmen spoke, and each began to work.

When Col was about to return to his translation work, he realized that Myuri was nowhere to be seen. He then remembered she had asked about breakfast. Perhaps she had not eaten all morning while waiting for him to wake up.

He hurriedly exited the room, and there was Myuri, leaning against the window frame in the hallway, gazing into the court-yard, and feeding the little birds.

"Myuri."

When he called to her, the birds suddenly flew away.

"Wow, the animals really hate you, Brother," said Myuri, with the blood of wolves flowing through her, and she bit into the bread in her hand that the birds had been pecking at.

"Your breakfast...Where did you get that bread?"

"I got it by dancing a little outside."

She wiggled her hips.

It seemed she was slightly angry with him.

"That was a joke."

"I know, however—"

"I have traveling money of my own. Here, this is for you."

She interrupted him, reaching into the bag dangling from her hand and pulling out crumbly, dry bread and jerky. She gave it to him.

"They called that a biscuit, and boatmen eat it. It's so hard, it'll break your teeth."

She grinned, showing off her canines. It certainly seemed hard enough, but that was not what he was concerned about.

"Ah, Myuri, I have work to do, so..."

"I know. It would definitely be weird if I were in the room with you."

She was the one who forced him to bring her along, so if she understood that there was no place for her and obediently returned to Nyohhira, it would be a great help.

"That's what's written on your face, at least."

"..."

"Well, I'm not going home."

She smiled mischievously and poked the chest of an unmoving Col.

"Now I know how Miss Helen and the others feel when they tease you, Brother."

How cheeky, he thought, glaring at her, and she took a step back.

"It's busy everywhere here, so I found work to do. Luckily, I get to wear this."

As she had yesterday, she was wearing the same clothes as the errand boys in the company.

However, her hair was in its usual state, which looked incredibly untidy when coupled with her outfit.

"If so, you must do your hair properly," he said, then added, "I'll braid your hair for you."

She probably had not braided her own hair on purpose.

"Heh-heh. Okay!"

She smiled happily and closed the distance between them. He felt she was doing as she pleased with him, but after a bit of thought, he decided it was fine as long as she was in a good mood.

As he braided her hair, boys who were cleaning and company employees carrying goods passed them several times, and they all stared at the two, confused by the odd sight of a guest braiding an errand boy's hair.

Col was most definitely embarrassed, and only the free-spirited Myuri was content and did not mind.

In the several days that followed, Col focused solely on his work.

There were very few things Col had to fix in the translation Hyland gave him, and it was rather a learning experience for him. The translation was further along in Winfiel itself, so if he did any translating himself, it would conflict with that. The task was awe-inspiring but also enjoyable. At any rate, he was free and would not lose anything, so he did as he pleased.

The scribes were also skilled, and the numbers of documents he received from Hyland increased. Without an illustrator decorating the margins, they could write five pages in a day. Out of the thirteen chapters of the scripture, Hyland gave him the manuscripts for the first four, and the number of copies grew and grew.

Whenever the scribes completed one, Hyland would take it and distribute it to the city nobles in Atiph and the land-owning nobles outside the urban area. There were also requests from the townspeople, and the day after distributing two parts of it, managers from each association clamored for a copy for themselves.

While Hyland's campaigning certainly helped, the town likely already had the groundwork for this result. It was frigid by the sea, and there were deep snow-covered mountains just up the river. According to the craftsmen, there had been pirate attacks from the stormy northern seas until recently. The environment outside the walls did not lend itself to a relaxing life, and the entire town thirsted for the teachings of God.

Such a situation allowed Col to work late into the evening, several nights in a row without distress. He had dedicated himself to studies that no one had ever found necessary until now. He would not consider any troubles he had to endure now as a hardship, as long as his efforts were of use later. The scribes left each day at sunset, but of course, he did not stop working then. Since he stayed up so late with the candle still burning, Myuri eventually forced him out at night. With no other choice, he placed a large crate and chair in the hallway, and then wrapped a blanket around himself as he worked to help him concentrate better.

Myuri made a point of being angry about it, but she was probably just cold sleeping by herself.

When he awoke, he could barely open his eyes—he was so happy thinking about the scripture that he did so even in his dreams. Back in Nyohhira, Lawrence understood him, but the work in the bathhouse was never-ending. This was the life Col had longed for.

But the single thing that disrupted his routine, whether in Nyohhira or Atiph, was of course Myuri. Once her work helping the company was finished, she would return to the room and tell him in detail about everything that happened that day. When he responded with disinterested grunts, she would finally fall quiet and instead pull up a chair beside his and read the scripture. Perhaps that was also because he would give actual answers to her questions about the translated portions.

However, as he pursued his work, Myuri grew worried about his health. That was to be expected since the food she prepared for him when she left in the morning was untouched when she got home.

Even though Col was usually the one to scold Myuri about her lifestyle habits, their positions were now completely flipped. She stopped shooing him out at night and instead began pulling him into bed as the candle burned low. It would be funny from an outsider's perspective, and he thought about how Myuri would make a good big sister if she had a younger sibling.

That being said, he figured his fervor for his work was difficult for Myuri to understand. One day, after pulling him from the desk into the bed again, she spoke.

"Hey, Brother? Can I ask you something?"

He tried to answer, but he coughed violently when he tried to speak, likely because he had not used his voice in a while. "What is it?" he finally managed to say.

"Why are you so obsessed with the teachings of God, Brother?"

Perhaps Myuri meant it as a reprimand, but it was a rather fundamental question.

"*Ahem*...Hmm. Have I never told you?"

"No. So...it's kind of scary."

She snuggled up to him and clung to his arm inside the blanket, perhaps out of fear that he would run back to the desk while she was sleeping. In reality, there were several times when he leaped out of bed as he was falling asleep after hitting upon a translation for a particular word that had escaped him.

But once he really thought about it, he had no memory of talking about this to Myuri. They had conversed about many things ever since she was a little girl, so it was a bit strange.

"I see...It is a difficult question, though. I might not be able to answer in a sentence or two."

"Tell me. If it satisfies me, then I'll set out two candles for you before I sleep."

It would not be bad to extend work hours by one candle. And if he could explain why he was so attached to the teachings of God, well, it would be a good opportunity to open Myuri's eyes to his lessons.

He slowly collected his thoughts and opened his mouth as he gazed up at the dark ceiling.

"I didn't believe the teachings of God and the Church at first."

"Really?!" Myuri yelled in his ear. She was as surprised as when she had first discovered that it cost money to boil water in the world beyond the hot springs of Nyohhira.

"Yes, really. The village I was born in was home to so-called pagans. We prayed to things like the beautiful springs or giant trees, and 'God' to us was a big frog, passed down through legend, that protected the village."

"A frog?"

"There was a legend about it. Perhaps it really existed a long time ago."

Myuri's mother was the embodiment of a giant wolf, after all.

"Well, that's where I was born, so I never honestly thought to learn about the teachings of the Church. It is ironic, but I decided I should learn when my village was about to be razed by their knights."

He recalled why he had never talked about this to Myuri. It was not an amusing story.

"The villages we interacted with disappeared one after another, and of course, there was nothing we could do. No matter how much we prayed to the village god, help never came. The adult men were prepared to fight until the bitter end, and women and children got ready to escape with the intention of never coming back."

A similar thing was probably happening somewhere in the world, but it was much more frequent back then. Myuri kept silent and gripped his arm even tighter. Her shoulders were hunched, as though she regretted asking him the story.

"Well, to jump to the end, coincidence after coincidence led to the village not being destroyed. It's still there today."

Myuri was clearly relieved.

"However, at the time, the entire northlands, which included my village, was called the pagan land. It was embroiled in a war."

"…Only Nyohhira was safe, right?"

At the time, the old lands of Nyohhira were called the paradise of true believers in the land of pagans.

"Right. That is why, regardless of whether or not the Church would attack us again, I figured there was only one way to protect the village. And that was to become an important person in the Church myself," he said, and Myuri was clearly at a loss.

Even he knew that it was a simple way of thinking.

"At the time, I…I was even more of an ignorant child than I am now. All my ideas were simple but at the same time calculating. Or perhaps strangely insolent. That's why, though I was learning about God's teachings then, my faith lay in the strength and ferocity of the organization that was the Church. The people around me who were studying the teachings also just wanted to have privileged work in the future, so no one seriously practiced them."

A university city was a bustling town where the wise men recognized by the Church as sages would congregate.

It cost money to study, and swindlers gathered wherever money was spent. There, all his savings were swept up, then he was burdened with debt, and in the end, he ran with his life.

It was a terrible experience, but thanks to that, he stood where he was now.

"But despite that, it must have suited my personality because I enjoyed learning about the teachings of God. Before I knew it, they became my flesh and blood, and once I had internalized them, the study itself became enjoyable. But no matter what, the thing called faith did not stick in my heart. That was because the world was too irrational and uncertain for me to carry that unwavering conviction."

There was a day when his village had been almost completely wiped out, a disaster prevented only by sheer luck, and then came the realization that the frog god they believed in only existed in their village—he had felt that there was nothing certain in this world.

He believed the only thing right in this world was that the strongest one would win.

"Those thoughts were completely overturned when I met two eccentric travelers."

"…Mother and Father?"

"That is correct."

Though it was a minor thing, Myuri seemed happy to hear the compliment. Her tail, which she used at night to keep herself warm, rustled under their blankets, and it tickled him.

"But…why? Wouldn't you think that the Church's God was a total lie after meeting Mother?"

There was likely no evidence against the existence of an even stronger god.

But his faith was of a completely different sort.

"Your thinking is correct. But in a way, not quite. While the ontological discussion of whether or not God truly does exist in heaven was important, the difference was that they taught me that there are things in this world to believe in from the bottom of my heart."

"…I don't get it."

Her tail moved under the covers, unsatisfied.

"If you assume that unshakable truths exist on this earth, don't you think their bond is one of them?"

The question seemed to startle Myuri. Then, after a moment's thought, she frowned slightly for some reason.

"Well, maybe. Mother and Father are so close it's gross." That was how she felt as their daughter. "But how is that related to God's teachings?"

"Well, let's see," he said and closed his eyes, recalling the big adventures he had had since meeting them—the exciting and sometimes dangerous times—and how he had still been able to laugh.

"No matter what danger they faced, even when they fell into hopelessness, they never let go of each other's hand. That is because they knew that their feelings for each other were the only certain thing in the world."

"..."

Myuri did not say anything, probably because it was embarrassing for her to hear such stories about her parents.

"When I watched them, I thought that as long as you had something to believe in, you could overcome any hardship. And then I learned that that 'something' most definitely existed. Looking around me with that in mind, I finally understood that faith was incredibly important to surviving in this cold world."

Faith could be feelings for a loved one, loyalty to the organization or lord that one served under, or even the less praiseworthy convictions of misers.

What they had in common, however, was that they could be strong because of their faith.

"And at the same time, I was painfully aware of the misery and powerlessness of the helpless, because I was once like that, too."

He could no longer fathom his despair from that time, nor did he want to. His loneliness had withered him away into nothing, like a malady pulling him into the abyss of death even as he lived.

"Then, for the first time, the teachings of a God flowed through my blood."

God was always with you.

He felt like the lid over his head opened when he finally understood it.

"When I understood the meaning of 'God will never abandon you,' it was like a warm waterfall suddenly washed over me."

He thought that Myuri might laugh at his exaggeration, but she surprisingly did not. On the contrary, she gripped his arm even tighter and rested her mouth on his shoulder as though she would bite it.

"I...get that. When you told me that you would always be my friend, I felt the same."

She sounded like she was sulking, perhaps because she was

131

being bashful. She was talking about the time when her mother, Holo, told her about the blood of wolves flowing through her veins.

"If I can become a priest, I would be able to spread that warmth throughout the world to all the people shivering in the cold of loneliness. When I was at such a loss as a child, I just so happened to run into Holo and Lawrence, but many people in the world will not have such luck. I realized, however, that I could be the one to bring that luck to those people. God's love is limitless and will not lessen when it's shared."

To that end, he had to understand God to the greatest extent possible. He had to be able to confront all sorts of doubts. He could dedicate himself to his studies, munching on raw onions to ward off sleepiness, because of his very faith.

"Um…," Myuri said, nonplussed, and Col was immediately apologetic that his speech might have been too intense.

"I'm sorry, that was fairly dramatic. But it is rather close, I think."

"No, that's not it…I was just surprised that you actually had a reason for studying. I was sure my brother was just a bit weird."

"Huh?"

He was slightly hurt, and when he looked at Myuri beside him, he could tell, especially through the darkness, that she was smiling mischievously.

"But now I understand. You really are weird if you think so seriously about that, and you never react when Miss Helen and the other dancers flirt with you, either."

"Myuri."

He lowered his voice to scold her, but Myuri continued on happily.

"And I think I understand a little why you left the village. I wasn't sure why you were so angry over whether or not the pope was collecting money…He's damaged something really important, hasn't he?"

That was exactly it. Her assessment was so accurate, he wanted to raise his voice in joy.

The pope was using the teachings of God that were meant as deliverance for the people as a tool in his desire for money. Col could not forgive such a thing.

"I am sad that I cannot express how happy I am right now that you've finally understood me."

"What? Then give me a big hug, like you used to when I was little."

She grew up to look exactly like her mother, Holo, then realized the appeal of decorating herself over chasing animals in the mountains—when he thought about how much she had grown, he felt sad. However, she was still a child on the inside.

He smiled as he thought that, and when he hugged her, she cackled.

"But, Brother?"

"What is it?"

"When Mother told me about my ears and tail and I cried, why didn't you tell me about such an important God?"

It was a given that the flow of their conversation would lead them here.

And the reason for that made him feel ill.

"Well, you see…"

"Yeah?"

If he lied to her now, Myuri would instead bully him to no end. He decided to resign himself to it.

"Even I have never seen God myself."

"Huh?"

"But *I'm* here. You can see me, touch me, and talk to me. That's why. It is…well…inconsistent…as a servant of God…"

There was nothing more shameful than this. Most of the deception of the Church must have been born from situations like this. As he thought surely Myuri would be dismayed, she spoke out of the blue.

"Just hug me again."

"What?"

"You can see and touch and talk to me, right? Hurry, before I lose all my faith!"

The day Myuri would develop a faith in God seemed far off, but perhaps that was a good thing, in a way.

He did as the princess commanded.

Either because she had been working hard or perhaps due to her usual skill, before long Col could hear the sounds of soft snoring coming from between his arms. She was always footloose and fancy-free. Though she was small, his arms quickly grew tired hugging her, unlike when she was a little girl. He let go, careful not to wake her, and breathed a sigh of relief.

He looked at her sleeping face once again, and his face spontaneously broke into a wide smile.

Perhaps it would be acceptable to add the innocence of this sleeping face to the list of things that were certain in this world.

It was a face that encouraged him to work hard tomorrow.

Col's days of prayer and contemplation continued, and as the copies of copies of Hyland's manuscript spread throughout town, Myuri finally caught up to where he had finished his work. She could not help but interfere with his business, deliberately rushing him on to work faster and faster, but he felt the same way.

When he finally finished translating the seventh chapter, he felt as though he was gasping for air and finally breathing again.

All the fundamental teachings found in the scripture lay within the first seven chapters, and the rest was about the travels of the prophets who had been given the words of God and the memoirs of their disciples. Of course, Col's translation was provisionary, and there were plenty of things that needed to be adjusted, but the general idea should have been communicated.

Then, he also felt relieved that he made it in time. Hyland, who had been running around laying the groundwork for the plan, just yesterday finally began serious talks with the archbishop at the Church.

From what he had heard, he imagined the town would be completely on the side of Winfiel Kingdom. A church built on the townspeople's respect as well as their donations surely could not ignore their wishes.

The first seven chapters of translated scripture that contained the basic teachings of God would unquestionably support this idea.

And his heart felt full when he thought about how the townspeople were so interested in God's teachings.

The world was not without worth. What was right was right, and the path would continue to the truth.

Long after the scribes returned home at dusk, he could somehow feel the last droplets of sunlight from the roof on the other side of the street.

"Brother! Are you done?"

Myuri was the only one who would open a door without knocking.

When he turned toward her, it felt like he was seeing her face for the first time in a long while.

"Didn't you say you'd be finished sometime today?"

"I did, just now."

"Good, good."

He could not help but smile as she spoke like a parent. "Have you learned a thing or two about hard work?"

"Of course. I've been doing so much every day. Everyone needs me everywhere. But what surprised me the most is how many jobs need to be done."

As Col checked the ink of the translation as it dried on the parchment, his heart relaxed at Myuri's enjoyment.

"Companies are the waterwheels that move the world, you know."

"There's lots of boring and tedious work, though."

"That's how it is."

"I know, but…I had to count the coins packed in these crates, and there were enough to drive me crazy! And there's *so* much money, and I spent all day counting it until my hands were black, but I only got a tiny, tiny, tiny bit of it!"

Now that he thought about it, there was indeed a night where she was particularly bothered by the smell on her hands. He had thought she touched a fish or something similar, but it seemed she was repelled by the smell of coin.

"But it's weird."

"Weird? What is?"

"The money changers had me running around doing errands for them, but they don't use any of that money."

"They might be keeping it safe for someone else or planning to use it for a large transaction. Perhaps for export."

"Export? You mean selling it to other towns? But everyone here is upset because there's no change, though."

"If there's a place that needs it more than they do here, then it would be more profitable to sell it there. It happens often."

"Huh. That's weird."

He wanted to brag that through that export of coin, he had discovered an incredible trick long ago, but he resisted since it was childish.

"Anyway, I don't want to do work like that. Work at the port is the most fun."

"The port?" he questioned, and Myuri's eyes lit up.

"They pile up cargo so high on big boats, and then you jump on top of it and throw everything down to people waiting for them on land. The port is packed with ships jostling together, and it's hard because they're always rocking back and forth when the waves come in! Especially today because a really skinny and long boat like a dragonfly came in around sunset and tried to force its way in, and because they didn't know the customs here, everyone shouted at one another!"

Myuri sniffed, puffing out her chest. She acted the part of a competent errand boy, already counting herself as a member of the Debau Company. She was an honest and energetic girl, and perhaps it helped her blend in easily around such places.

When she mentioned a boat that looked like a dragonfly, she was likely referring to the quick ones that did not depend on the wind and were instead propelled forward by man power with dozens of oars lined up on either side. Perhaps there had been cargo that required urgent delivery.

Setting that aside, he briefly imagined her jumping onto the tall mountains of cargo in the noisy port.

"Erm…Isn't that rather dangerous?"

"Yeah, lots of people fell into the sea. I'm the only one who didn't!"

Myuri spoke proudly. In Nyohhira, she was fine jumping from creek to creek to play beside icy rapids. Of course, she was a skilled swimmer.

But that was not the problem.

"I am looking after you in place of Lawrence and Holo. If you happen to get hurt, what will you do?"

"Oh, I know. If I become damaged goods, then someone has to take responsibility."

"..."

He breathed a heavy sigh. She was acting knowledgeable about the things Miss Helen and the other dancers told her, even though she did not understand.

"I meant something a little different, but...that's roughly correct."

"Really?"

As soon as she said that, there came the sound of a mooing cow.

"More importantly, I'm hungry. Oh, can you go out now that you're finished working?"

Col had been eating in the room for these past few days. Myuri seemed to want to eat things they did not have in Nyohhira that could be found in the busier parts of town. But when it was apparent that he would not budge, she had obediently had someone from the company buy her a meal before eating her bread and other foodstuffs in the room.

"Yes, yes, very well. It's been a while since I've moved my body; it feels like if I don't, then I might just become stone."

"There were so many times I actually thought you died."

Myuri cackled, and she suddenly raised her head as though she had realized something.

"Oh, Brother!"

"What is it?"

"Since we're going out, you shouldn't dress like that," she said, and he looked down at himself, but nothing had changed since he left Nyohhira.

He pressed his hand against his cheek to check if there was something on his face, but Myuri shook her head in a fit.

"Get rid of that priest-looking coat."

"What?"

"Just do it!"

He did as he was told and removed the coat, and Myuri carefully inspected him from head to toe before groaning.

"But you still kind of look like it..."

"Myuri? What are you talking about?"

"Brother, put your head down."

It was too much trouble to ask again, so as he did as he was told and lowered his head, she roughly ruffled his hair.

"...Myuri."

"How about this...? Oh! This might work!"

After glancing around, she opened the pot of ink, dipping the tip of her pinkie into it and drawing a quick line on his cheek. She did the same on the other side and then stepped back to examine him.

"Well, whatever."

"Myuri."

There was a hint of anger in his voice, but Myuri did not flinch, placing both hands on her hips and puffing out her chest.

"It's dangerous to walk around outside dressed like a priest now."

"...What?"

"All the men that do heavy labor are all worked up."

As the curtains of night drew over the sunset, Myuri's eyes glinted threateningly in the faint darkness.

"During breaks at work, I've been collecting all sorts of information from the townspeople. I've been working hard."

"All sorts...?"

"We're dividing up the work! You're working hard here in the room, but you won't know what's going on in the outside world. So instead, I'm your eyes and ears! Isn't that adventure basics?"

His only response was a blank stare, and Myuri's expression changed to one of clear displeasure.

"You really didn't think I was working just to amuse myself because I was bored, did you?"

"No..."

He had been absolutely certain that was the case.

"Sheesh! See, this is why I say you're no good! You have no idea what that blondie is scheming!"

Of course, Col did not think that people of high status such as Hyland acted for simple reasons.

However, Myuri's thorough distrust in him seemed to go beyond that.

"You're really only looking at a fourth of the world, Brother."

"Not even half?"

The world was made up of men and women. It appeared he did not know a thing about women, so that left a half. Even if he woefully accepted this evaluation of himself, where did that second half come from?

Then, Myuri's expression became troubled yet slightly sad, and she spoke.

"You only ever look at the good parts of people."

This innocent and naive girl sometimes dug into deep places.

"But people aren't bundles of goodwill. Right?"

It was a cold truth. If Myuri, who was half his age, had to tell him this, then perhaps he truly was only seeing less than a fourth of the world.

As he stared vacantly, she placed her warm hand on top of his.

"But I could never imagine you doing anything evil, Brother."

He gazed down at her, and the girl who was always doing evil things was giggling.

"So I'm going to protect you. I'll keep an eye out where you're not looking and make sure you don't fall backward off a cliff."

He thought for a moment how cheeky she sounded, but she had saved him from being run over by a wagon when he had been too caught up in his thoughts.

He could not think of anything to say in return, but it was beneath him to stay silent.

"Then, what should I be looking at with my narrow field of vision?"

Myuri gave him a sidelong glance before shaking her head in exasperation.

"Isn't there someone you can't take your eyes off of?"

Her usage of that phrase was a bit off, but she was much too proud of herself.

That discrepancy was funny to him, and he could not help but smile.

"Of course."

"Of course!"

She grinned, baring her teeth. Then, she placed her forehead on his arm.

"That's why..."

"Huh?"

Her voice was muffled, and he could not hear her, but by the time he asked for clarification, she had already let go of his arm.

"More importantly, I'm hungry!"

He got the sense that she said something important to him but also that she had rubbed her nose against him mostly to satisfy an itch. At any rate, it was true that he could not take his eyes off her.

"Don't eat too much."

"Okay."

Her noncommittal response was typical.

He followed her as she quickly exited the room, a slight smile of exasperation on his face.

The energy of the town at night was different from how it was during the day.

It was more similar to Nyohhira's—a feast of drink and meat.

Unlike in the sleepy hot spring village, though, sturdy, muscular men sat on long benches that jutted out onto the roads, making a ruckus. They were probably the men who unloaded cargo at the docks, craftsmen who cut wood with big saws, or the workers who braided the ferociously thick ropes that tied the largest ships to the piers. The men, baked in salt and alcohol, had piercing laughs and yells that carried a particular kind of impact.

Then, Col understood immediately that Myuri's earlier caution was correct.

"So what's the archbishop gonna do?"

"An assistant priest was the only one who showed up to prayer this morning. They're so scared of Lord Winfiel!"

"No, no, the archbishop and Lord Winfiel were meeting the whole time inside the church."

Everyone was talking about the Church and the Kingdom of Winfiel—namely, Hyland. Some were simply observing the course of events, while others bellowed their disdain for the Church's taxes and called Hyland a savior.

Col and Myuri watched the revelers as they strolled along, and at the food stalls that were still out even after sunset, Col bought sandwiches containing a slice of cod that was deep-fried in oil. Myuri must have earned some spending money while she worked during the day because she pulled out some coins from her wallet and bought sausage, too.

"If I had come out dressed as I was, I definitely would not have been able to eat."

He could imagine drunks catching him and closing in on him, asking whose side he was on.

"Appearance is important."

You see? Myuri asked wordlessly with a tilt of her head. Once he smiled and nodded in response, he nudged her in the head.

As they stood on a corner of the street, eating their bread and watching people come and go, Col came to understand several things.

He learned what the men were interested in and what they talked about. Some showed the others that there were copies of a vernacular translation of the scripture. They raised cries of awe, as if declaring that was all they would need to defeat the malpractices of the Church.

These people were drunk, of course, so Col could not accept their words and actions at face value. However, he could see the extent of their expectations. If all these townspeople were on his side, then Hyland's wishes would surely come true. Given all this, the archbishop could not ignore the wishes of the populace. He would need to work to correct the misdeeds, then join them in raising his voice against the pope.

"We might be able to achieve justice at this rate."

Starting with the Church in Atiph, the movement would link to the next town, then the next. Col could not help but feel excited when he imagined his work helping this along.

He looked out on the town from the street corner with a hope-filled gaze, and Myuri, blending in with the scenery of the town as she leaned against the wall and nibbled at her bread, sighed.

"Justice…justice?"

"What's the matter? Isn't everyone facing the right direction, like Heir Hyland is?"

After Col asked his question, Myuri regarded him expressionlessly before jerking her chin like a real errand boy would.

Wondering what it was, he turned in the direction she indicated and found some rowdy men sitting on the benches of the bars along the street.

"Ha-ha-ha!"

"Here, here, look, look!"

He could hear jeers along with the barking of a dog. A drunk had jerky in his hands and was teasing a stray. That itself was not peculiar. The settlement was brimming with animals inside the walls.

"Here, it's tithe meat! Go on and eat it up!"

He threw the jerky, and the dog ran after it at full speed and ate it. The men watched, guffawing. Then Col noticed something odd about the dog.

Someone had put a cloth around its neck to make it look like a priest.

"Father Dog! Please take our tithe bread, too!"

Every time the dog ate the food, the men would double over in laughter.

There was a half smile on Myuri's face, but Col could not smile at all.

It was a clear desecration of authority.

"They've been like that since yesterday. I'm used to people drinking and getting unruly at Nyohhira, but they're completely different. It's a little...scary."

Myuri finished eating her bread and brushed off the crumbs on her clothes.

"During the day today, a pastor from a church on a nearby island came. It was awful then, too."

"In what way?"

The dog received its food with delight. The more it wagged its tail, the harder the men laughed.

"I think it's a rule that the boats of important people from the Church have the Church's insignia on the sail, unpainted. So everyone knew immediately what kind of person was aboard. Then came loud applause and loud cheers."

He glanced at her, and her expression was dark. Her countenance did not match her story.

Or perhaps Myuri would rather the pastor not be welcomed?

As he considered this, the good-looking errand boy sighed.

"No one had come to welcome him. The people from the company told me this, but apparently, he was called to support the archbishop, and since the town is hostile against the Church, he would be opposing that blondie. Everyone knew, so they greeted him with fake cheers and applause. There was no way they could turn the boat back, either. So when he was getting off the ship, the pastor hesitated and went pale. Like he knew he'd come at a bad time."

Malice.

It was malice boiling up in opposition to authority.

"No one was really welcoming him, and it was scary to think he might be mobbed. That pastor seemed to be a nice man, and when he left the port, it looked like he was running away."

Not everyone rested on their laurels in privilege. That was true even for the archbishop in this town. He was ardent in his holy work, so he was not a wholly bad person.

"After working here for a few days, I noticed that no one really cares about the details. I don't know—it's hard to explain, but it feels like that as long as there's something to get riled up about, they'll go for anything. Everyone is so mad, saying things like,

'How dare they take our money away!' When I ask if the tithes are really that expensive, they laugh and tell me they've never been taxed by the tithes."

Surely it was impossible that each and every person who spent the day carrying cargo would be compelled to pay such a tax. That tax took money from things such as large companies, checkpoints, or land revenue. Of course, it was possible to think that the tithe would at some point affect the little people, but it would be difficult for those individuals to actually feel its effects.

"Hey, Brother. You know what you believe, and you looked like you were really enjoying yourself, concentrating on your translation work, so I didn't say anything."

There was a degree of sincerity in the eyes gazing up at him that he had never seen in her before.

"Copies of your translation are circulating, too, and it's like it's okay to insult the Church any way they like now that they have that."

"That was not what the translation was—"

"It seems like it doesn't really matter what you think or what's written on it."

Details like God's word did not matter. There were even merchants who, when they saw him carrying out his daily task of recitation of the scripture, thought it good luck and bowed their head for protection. That was normal.

"So you really have to be careful. That blondie might have acted knowing this would happen."

"That's…"

"Nothing comes out of that mouth but good things."

Only half of half of the world.

He stared hard back at Myuri, but he could not respond. When he averted his eyes, he could see the dog that was being teased.

Had he been too naive? But faith was an innocent thing. If innocence and naïveté were bad, then what should he do?

Certainly, Col did not think that Hyland was acting entirely on saintly motives. However, he was sure righteousness lay at the end of their path.

The feeling left him uncertain of everything.

He wanted so desperately to read the scripture.

"Myuri."

"Hmm?"

He spoke as he watched the dog being baited while the men roared with laughter.

"Let's return to the trading house."

He was not translating the scripture for the sake of such ill will. He did not want to make a fool of the Church's authority. He simply wanted to state that there were inconsistencies and then rectify them.

Of course, these sorts of people did not represent everyone, and he could not imagine Hyland was egging them on. But still, it made him realize that he was only looking at a quarter of the world.

"Okay."

He had expected she might make a fuss, wanting to buy more to eat, but she responded easily.

She separated herself from the wall and was about to walk off, but she twirled around to face him.

"Do you want me to hold your hand?"

Col had worked hard for his ideals but then found unforeseen malice in the townspeople. Perhaps his disappointment was visible on his face. Myuri was teasing him while making sure he was all right.

He could not tell which one of them was supposed to be older.

"...It's not my fault if I get lost," he said.

"Hey!"

Myuri pulled him along as they went back the way they came.

She walked quickly, likely because she wished to pull him out of the vulgar atmosphere of town as soon as possible. Though she was noisy, selfish, and sometimes said such terrible things that astonished him, she was a good girl.

And his line of thinking continued.

If Myuri was such a good girl, then it would not be odd to find others who were just as good.

Col knew that once one began doubting the world, there was no end to it, and he understood that there were bad people. In fact, his meeting Lawrence came about when he had just been swindled by a crook.

So while some made a fool of the Church's authority simply in order to lighten their mood, most people would read the common-language version of the scripture and understand both the Church's righteousness and sins. At least, that was what he wanted to believe.

Col and Myuri returned to the trading house and headed up toward the third floor, weaving through the people who were still working at this hour.

"You can do what you want, but today you have to sleep properly! Okay?!"

"Yes, yes."

He smiled at Myuri as she howled at him and opened the door. Then the smell of ink enveloped him, easing the anxiety in his heart from the commotion outside.

The scent was that of knowledge and tranquility.

"I'd like to wash my face before sleeping, however. And Myuri, you smell like dirt, so please go get some water—"

As he spoke and lit the candle, he finally noticed that Myuri had stopped in the doorway.

"Myuri?"

She did not respond to him, and as he thought he saw her shivering, her ears and tail appeared. Then, she entered the room and closed the door, sniffing.

He thought it must be some sort of joke, but as though drawn in by an invisible string, she walked in a straight line and stopped before the desk.

"Myuri."

It was not a question but a call. The manuscript of the translation he had just finished was stacked neatly on the desk. Nothing had changed most likely since before they left the room.

"Someone was here while we were gone. Many 'someones.'"

However, there was no denying the tension in the bristling hair on Myuri's tail and ears.

In addition, this room did not lock. Anyone could come and go as they pleased.

"Could someone have stolen something?"

He turned the bundle of parchment over, shining a candle over it to check. However, the number of pages was correct, and the handwriting was his own.

"It has not been marked over…Perhaps someone came to read purely out of interest?"

There were fervent believers within the company. They had likely heard a rumor that the translation would be finished soon and come to read it, but no one was here, so they instead read it on their own because they could not wait.

As he contemplated, Myuri, who had bent over to sniff around the desk, stood up and rubbed her nose.

"I don't know. All I know is that someone was here. If I could be a wolf like Mother, then I might be able to tell who," Myuri said regretfully and sneezed.

While she could hide and show her ears and tail at will, she could not become a giant wolf like her mother, Holo. That was perhaps because she also had human blood.

"Anyway, you need to be careful, okay?"

"I will. However, I do not think it would be wise to doubt people too much."

Myuri waved her tail slowly, frowning at Col when he insisted, arms still folded.

Then he sighed and shrugged, as though surrendering.

"Well then, I will go retrieve hot water…Just in case, stick my short sword into the floor and use the hilt to keep the door shut."

"If we're going through that much effort, then I'm coming with you."

She sounded angry, and he considered that was also an option.

He placed the lit candle onto a handheld stand and was about to leave the room.

"Oh, someone just came up to the third floor. I think these are Lewis's footsteps," Myuri said as her ears twitched. That was likely the name of another errand boy she had made friends with as she worked. When he thought that they might as well ask for water while they were at it, she suddenly hid her ears and tail. There was a knock at the door only a few moments later.

"Pardon me for intruding while you rest."

There came a proper greeting. This person was probably not whoever came into the room while they were gone and did as they pleased.

"Come in," Col responded. The door opened, and there was a boy about two or three years older than Myuri.

"Pardon me. Heir Hyland has called for you."

When he said that, Col realized that Hyland was perhaps the one who had visited. As his client, he had the right to read the completed product whenever he pleased, and doubtless he did not think much of going into a commoner's room without permission.

"Very well. We shall go posthaste," he replied, and the boy bowed his head respectfully. Col saw him look inside the room. The boy's composed expression turned into a smile, and he gave a little wave.

Of course, Col was kind enough to pretend he did not notice.

They closed the door, and Myuri grinned as she leaned against the desks the scribes used.

"Was that Lewis?"

"Yeah. We were at the port together, and he fell into the sea twice."

He could not tell for sure if she was smiling because they were close or because she was recalling how silly he was for falling into the sea. Perhaps both.

"Well then, I will be going to Heir Hyland, so..."

He purposefully trailed off.

"I'm going, too."

"There might not be any candy this time."

"It's fine. If you feed me too much, I might not be able to see anything else."

In reality, perhaps Hyland enjoyed giving candy to Myuri as much as taming a cautious beast in the mountains.

"You cannot do anything rude."

"Okay."

She left the desk and exited the room first.

As he was about to follow her, he suddenly turned back to face the room.

Would it be all right to simply leave the translation manuscript as it was?

"Brother?"

Myuri called to him from the hallway, and after a moment of hesitation, he decided to bring it with him.

At any rate, he had to announce that he had finished translating everything up to the seventh chapter.

"Sorry to keep you waiting."

"Yeah. Since I got blueberries and apples last time, I guess pears are next."

He smiled at Myuri's gluttony as she forecasted what candy would be available and began walking.

But at the end of the long hallway, beyond the reach of the light in his hands, there was a deep darkness.

There was no harm in being careful.

He amended his opinion as they headed to Hyland.

Hyland had summoned them long after night had fallen. Moreover, he had begun talks with the archbishop just the day before.

He presumably had many reasons for calling on them.

"Oh, there you are."

Once they were let into the room, Hyland greeted them from a table with a blindingly white cloth draped over it. Food sat on it, but it seemed like it had gone cold a while ago.

"I am sorry; we were out eating."

"It's fine." Hyland smiled wryly, fiddling with a knife. "I'm not very hungry."

He let go of the knife and leaned back in the chair.

"I'm sure you are strained under negotiations. Please do not push yourself."

"Strained…I don't think that's quite it. Maybe unwell or disappointed."

Hyland's choice of words did not bode well for the negotiations.

"Is the archbishop being stubborn even with the townspeople's support?"

Then, Hyland gave a slight laugh.

"The townspeople's support, huh?"

Col could tell that Myuri, standing beside him, was falling into a sour mood. There was a slight sneer to Hyland's smile. However, that was not meant for them.

"I thought so, too. But the ones making noise are all of the lower class."

Cargo men at the dock, fishermen, and day laborers.

"And those like them know nothing except how to clamor violently. Today, a pastor under the archbishop was called in to support him, but when he arrived at the church, he sank to the floor. The man was terrified, as if he had just fled a battlefield."

That was likely the pastor whom Myuri had talked about before—the one who was greeted with applause and cheers in a place he was not welcome.

"Do you know how they see me now as a result of that?" Hyland lamented, sitting tiredly in front of the food that had long gone cold. "They think I am trying to incite a civil war and annex this town into the kingdom."

"What?"

This was completely unrelated to the fighting between the Kingdom of Winfiel and the pope.

"Are you aware some are posting the translation of the scripture around town and waving it about? Because of that, the archbishop shouted at me, claiming that the translation was false and it was actually literature to incite a revolt."

"No…"

"Of course, anyone can see it's real by reading it. I even presented it to the archbishop. But since they presume that the symbol of the town's authority will lead our revolution, all the important people here are hesitant. On the off chance his judgment was actually true, then supporting me would be taking the side of a rebel."

Hyland spoke in a self-deprecating way, and there was pain in his slight smile.

In addition, the courteousness of Stefan, who directed this Debau Company trading house, was keeping Hyland at a more respectful distance rather than offering respect itself. They conducted trade here, and it was more profitable for them not to challenge the authorities.

Along that vein of thinking, he felt he had an idea of who might have come into their room to read the translation manuscript while they were out. It must have been someone from the Debau Company who came to check and make sure he was not writing an essay in that room that called for revolution.

Hyland inhaled deeply before a long and slow exhale.

"Back home, more and more people are losing God's protection at each major turning point in their lives, thanks to the pope. It's not that we don't believe in God. It's not that we are using this opportunity to take over territories of other countries. We are simply unsatisfied with how the pope is placing God's protection and money on the same scale. I don't understand...how he can't comprehend such simple logic."

He tightened his fist, and it shook on the table. Col understood his dismay and did the same.

However, when Hyland finally relaxed his fist, there was an embarrassed smile on his face.

"Or perhaps, he is trying to rile me up. The moment you become angered is the moment you lose. Especially in negotiations."

Hyland reached out to his drink, took a sip, then spoke.

"It was the same in the discussion with the archbishop in

Lenos. He lined up all the people he could and had them all throw any insult they liked at me. That makes even the darkest things seem light."

Church authorities could not remove Hyland by force, so instead they used the tyranny of the majority.

"And so, Col. I have something to ask of you."

"Of me?"

"I want to increase my numbers, even by a little. I don't know if he will try the same strategy tomorrow, but I want you to come with me to the negotiations."

Col was about to respond to this unexpected result, but Hyland stopped him with a smile.

"I may ask for theological advice, but I won't ask you to speak actively. I just want you to be there for dignity's sake. I've told him that you are a young and accomplished scholar who keeps company with famous theologians. It should be effective enough if you simply stand there with a stern expression. The archbishop would never quiz you on the scripture. They did not reach their posts through the teachings of God but gained their seats navigating secular society."

It seemed Hyland's impression had formed after actually talking to them rather than mere prejudice.

"And even though the archbishop has never actually read the scripture, this is a port town. He would know the names of famous priests who pass by on their way to and from Nyohhira. If we mention some of their names and characteristics and talk as though you have a mentor, then perhaps the priests may consider you the equal of renowned theologians."

Col felt like a scarecrow trying to chase off birds from the new shoots in a field, but he would do anything as long as it would help.

"I really don't want to use such an awkward strategy. It seems, however, that the wonderful world in which people recognize their own folly upon hearing the truth only exists in books."

Hyland seemed to be wearing down thanks to the gap between ideals and reality.

But at the mention of books, Col remembered he had a bundle of ideals in his own hands.

"By the way, about the translation, I've completed a provisional draft of everything up to the seventh chapter."

"Oh!"

Hyland's face suddenly brightened, and that made Col happy, too.

"I'm sure it will need editing, but I think the general idea comes across well."

"No, thank you for your hard work."

Col handed him the parchment, and Hyland skimmed the words with an affectionate expression.

"Mm...Ah, this is good."

It was most certainly lip service, but Col allowed himself a bit of pride as a reward.

"I'm sorry I don't have time to read it all. How much of this has been copied so far?"

"The copies reach about halfway through the seventh chapter. I just finished the rest of the chapter today, so I think I can copy it by morning. I'll give that to the scribes so when we bring this part to the Church, they can continue to make copies."

"Thank you for such quick thinking. Can you do that for me?"

"Of course."

After taking back the parchment from Hyland, Col found hope in the steady progress and future prospects for their work.

"This is a historical first step, the opening move to provide people with the ability to read the scripture and realize what is right. I'm counting on you, Col."

Col accepted Hyland's encouragement and left the room.

Col ended up staying up by the candle that night, but Myuri was not angry. She did not send him out, but instead carefully read the translation beside him as he made copies. It was a fleeting hope of his that she would finally awaken to God's teachings. She was perhaps unhappy that he had been given work once again, maybe because she was being neglected or maybe because she did not fancy Hyland.

When she suddenly rested her head on his shoulder as they worked, the gesture was also an expression of discontent.

The typically noisy girl was able to finish reading the entire translation without saying a single word.

When she lifted her head, she stretched and yawned, checking his progress. Once she saw that he still had a while to go, she stood up without saying anything in particular and headed straight for bed.

He thought about how she always did as she liked; her actions did suggest she was a little angry. After tomorrow, he had to find some time to spend with her.

When the idea crossed his mind, he was astonished at his own mollycoddling, but it was like an unbreakable habit now.

He imagined that if they were to part, not only would that mean he would no longer work at the bathhouse, but also that there would be a small hole in his heart.

It did not take until morning for Col to finish copying the rest of the translation, and he did so around the time when the town had fallen completely silent.

He could not be yawning in the middle of serving as Hyland's companion, so Col slept, warmed by the heat of Myuri's tail. He woke up at sunrise anyway. Myuri, who only stirred when the sun had risen well above the horizon, was completely exasperated when she heard about his early rising. But even Col realized it was all because he was too excited.

The scribes eventually came, and Col handed them a copy of the remaining translation. Once that was finished, he told them to give the copies to anyone who wanted them. He would take the original translation with him and Hyland to the church.

"And why are you wearing that?"

Myuri was dressed in her clothes from when they left Nyohhira, and her cape rested on her shoulders. Though it had only been a few days, she seemed more grown-up when she dressed femininely.

Perhaps because she had been working in town.

"Why? Because if I went to the church dressed like a company errand boy, it wouldn't be good for the business, would it? We talked about it yesterday."

Even if the Debau Company wanted to support Hyland, Stefan, who ran this trading house, did not want to oppose the Church. In addition, people were wondering if the crude commotion was as a result of the fighting from the territory annexation.

Myuri's judgment was indeed correct, but he had to question her use of it as a premise.

"Is waiting in the room like a good girl not an option?"

"No! I already read the scripture. I don't think I'd learn anything new if I kept working."

"Is it because I can only see a fourth of the world?" he said, and after Myuri stared at him blankly, she laughed, tickled.

"Yep."

"Honestly...I don't know what Heir Hyland will say."

There was slight hope in his words, but when they went to Hyland's room, it went over surprisingly well.

"That look is not quite acceptable, but if you take off the corset and wear the errand boy trousers, then wrap the sash around your waist, yes. You would pass for the apprentice of a court official. I can get a hat with a quill ready while we're at it. You have a well-groomed and open face. Any sort of look would fit you."

Hyland only seemed slightly amused by this, but when she actually wore the clothes and tied her hair roughly at the nape of her neck, Col agreed that it would not be odd if she truly did work under a noble.

"Looks are important."

"Exactly."

When Hyland agreed with her, Myuri snorted proudly.

"Then let us go. The morning prayers have finished, and people will be exiting the church and heading to work at the stores or workshops."

Hyland and his attendants had a carriage prepared for them, but Col and Myuri would follow on foot. The roads were always crowded, and if they were unlucky, then it would actually be faster to walk. Besides, they would also get a better feel for the atmosphere in town.

There was nothing left of the rough scene they had witnessed last night, and the town of Atiph was shimmering under the light of the sun. When Col looked out across these sights, he almost wanted to believe it was all a bad dream he'd seen in the darkness.

It was poor etiquette for a carriage to stop in front of the church if there was no official event, so Hyland had swung around to the back. There were young assistant priests, their sleeves rolled up and hands red from washing.

They were scrubbing the walls of the church with worn rags.

"Good morning. Is the archbishop in?" Hyland called, and one assistant priest, who seemed a little older than Myuri with a beard that had not quite grown in yet, wiped his hands and reticently opened the back door. It was a rough, steel gate that could stop the advances of enemies when the time called for it.

"Pardon us."

As Hyland passed them, the assistant priests lowered their gazes, but when his attendants and Col himself followed, they glared openly. The group entered the dim church, and the back door shut with a heavy thud behind them. Myuri whispered to him.

"They really don't want us here."

"They must be irritated that they have to do extra work this morning."

Hyland was the one that answered.

"Is cleaning not good practice, though?" Col asked.

"It depends on what they're cleaning up."

Col tilted his head at the answer, and Myuri whispered in his ear. "Rotten eggs."

His gaze unwittingly snapped back to her. There were no shops on the streets behind the church, and few people were around during the night. He could easily imagine unsatisfied individuals bringing in rotten eggs. From the perspective of the Church, Hyland was the one stirring those people up, so of course he and his hangers-on were not welcome.

They briskly strode straight through the church. It was not a form of insolence or audacity, but rather due to the risk of being thrown out if they did not, or possibly being forced to wait indefinitely in a room somewhere if they politely asked for directions.

The church felt bigger than it looked from the outside, and the stone buildings were indeed impressive. Huge, imposing scarlet tapestries hung from the wall, and stone-carved candlestands formed neat rows—it was the epitome of luxury. The lights at night were most likely beeswax instead of tallow.

When they finally reached the office, Hyland swung open the double door without hesitation.

Then, he took a step forward and spoke.

"Good morning. I thank God for the privilege of seeing you again today."

The space was large and the ceiling was high. The room was longer than it was wide, and the longest table Cold had ever seen, one that could easily fit twenty people, sat in the middle of the room. Along the walls were wooden shelves and oblong chests with elaborate designs, and on the plastered walls above them were pictures of angels, twelve in total, all bigger than the one he had seen in the Debau Company. Even the drawing rooms in the largest companies were not this luxurious.

There were seven pastors sitting at the table, all wearing purple robes with striking needlework, and two secretaries with parchment spread out before them. At the head of the table, sitting beneath the large crest of the Church painted on the wall, was the archbishop wearing robes embroidered with gold.

Behind them stood two or three chamberlains, each waiting. They were either assistant priests who did odd tasks as they studied God's teachings or secular secretaries who worked in administration for the Church's council. Surely, if all of them yelled together, any argument no matter how sound would be snuffed out.

"Glory be to God," the archbishop chanted, but his expression was sour. "You've brought quite the entourage."

He immediately began with a jab, but Hyland smiled delicately as he sat down in the chair a servant had pulled out for him.

"The more people, the warmer this room will be."

The archbishop, still frowning, exhaled loudly through his nose.

"By the way, the translation of the scripture finally reached the seventh chapter today. I would like to give this manuscript to you."

Hyland gave a signal, and a waiting servant took the parchment and brought it over to the priests.

There was not a single friendly countenance among any of the priests, but the waiting chamberlains politely presented the document to the archbishop.

"Perhaps reading it for yourself will convince you that it is not an essay of revolt rather than simply hearing it from me. Of course, God does not like conflict, and we are advocating harmony."

The archbishop turned a page of the parchment before him and looked up.

"May I read this?"

"Of course."

Hyland's voice sounded slightly animated. Col was a little surprised as well. He was sure the archbishop would not even spare a glance. He quickly read the first page, carefully reading every word, then turned to the second page. He read cautiously and silently.

As he did so, not a single word came out of the thirty or so people in the large office. Occasionally, someone's idle stirring or coughing would make a sound. The archbishop's gaze was fixed onto the parchment, and he did not look up.

Col thought something was strange, as he was spending an abnormal amount of time on the second page.

"Is something the matter?"

When Hyland spoke, the archbishop turned the page and proceeded to the third. What a coincidence that he had finally finished reading it just then. Again, he spent an abnormal amount of time on the third page.

Col looked at Hyland and noticed his profile had stiffened in anger.

He finally realized that they had been tricked.

The archbishop suspected that the translation of the scripture was literature to incite a revolt, and to prove their innocence, they had him read it. Therefore, he should read it to the end, but to him, there was no need. The one with something to lose if the discussions failed was Hyland.

It would be no use for them to request he read faster, and it would be just as he wanted if they grew angry at his slow pace.

For him, it would be cause for celebration if they got up from their chairs in defeat. This was no longer a negotiation, because the archbishop would not listen in the first place. Hyland's words were much too accurate—they were not sitting in those seats thanks to the teachings of God, but by navigating secular society.

The office was simply quiet, but the atmosphere was oppressive. Hyland's noble dignity did not waver, and with one arm on the table, he stared at the archbishop. It was as though he was staring at a rat that would escape the moment he averted his gaze.

However, Col did not know what they would do about this stalemate. He could not imagine that the archbishop would finish reading. They could not request that he do so. They could not stand up. They were completely trapped.

He recalled the story of the failure in Lenos. The archbishop there must have done the same thing to Hyland. The young man was Col's equal when it came to theological debates but, also like himself, unused to the spite of society.

He thought about this and yet was ashamed and irritated that there was nothing he could do.

When he began to wonder how much time had passed, he heard the ringing of a bell coming from outside the office. It sounded like the one in the church's bell tower, signaling midday. That made him realize that no matter how deadlocked the situation inside the office might be, outside, people were living their lives normally, and time was flowing. He wondered if Hyland was betting on that flow.

As the night went on, that vulgar and violent time would come once again. Drunk men would dress dogs in priests' clothes and ridicule their authority. Meanwhile, rational-seeming merchants, holding chicken thighs and scraps of the scripture translation, would spout insults at the Church as they ate their meat.

And still, the scribes were copying the translation back at the Debau Company trading house and distributing it. Those with good sense would read it and immediately understand that there was no righteousness in the Church's tyranny. Those people might then throw eggs not at the back door, but at the church's front gates. Once the people stood up to correct the Church's evil ways, Hyland would wait for the right time to brandish his sword for the negotiations.

Then, when he thought about it that way, Col began to see the archbishop's plan. It was possible he was betting on the complete opposite.

According to all the stories Myuri had heard as she did menial work for the company, the rowdy workers were simply lashing out because they could. It had nothing to do with the righteousness of faith or because the heavy tithes were weighing them down. Their troublemaking was nothing but a temporary fad, and if nothing came of it, then it was easy to imagine that their attention would simply go elsewhere.

165

The season was changing from winter to spring, and the busiest season of the year quickly approached. That much was obvious given the number of people visiting the Debau Company to petition. Soon the calendar would be full of spring festivals and religious ceremonies, so the archbishop would be running many of these things as his religious duty and would not lack excuses for pushing Hyland's negotiations back.

Religious work was like salt—the Church's presence was indispensable in daily life, especially during the change of seasons and important events throughout one's life. If Hyland's goals somehow hindered this work, then those who bore him ill will would undoubtedly appear. The very reason the people of the Winfiel Kingdom were suffering in the first place was because of that cessation of religious rites.

Would the people first raise their voices in anger, or would their interests return to their day-to-day?

Col thought silently in the nervous, oppressive atmosphere. This was a fight for how he should believe in the world. The people would see what was right and stand up for it. At the very least, that was what he and Hyland believed.

Oh God, he prayed.

But he did not know if it was correct to pray that the archbishop, a servant of God himself, was wrong. Heaven and earth had switched, and he was dizzy. Like the boat captain had said, the river did not flow in a straight line.

Though one could claim that such was the way of the world, his simple life in Nyohhira still felt so far away.

Time passed so slowly and painfully it seemed to chip away at him. Neither Hyland nor the archbishop spoke, so nobody suggested lunch. Time continued to pass, and the light shining through the skylight near the top of the high ceiling was now on the other side of the room from when they entered.

His legs and lower back were in pain, and it was likely that everyone there felt the same way. Not just the ones standing, but those sitting as well. Simply sitting in a chair was just as bad for the body. The older priests were noticeably exhausted. On the other hand, Hyland's side was all young people, including himself. The chamberlains behind the priests were also young, but it appeared Hyland's side had the advantage in this contest of endurance.

The one Col was worried about was Myuri, but she had the strength to run around in the mountains, so she was somehow enduring this. But when it crossed his mind that she may not come the next day, it almost made him smile.

Eventually, the light coming through the skylight began lengthening, and the color deepened. As he surmised that everyone must be thinking about the approaching end of the day, a loud sound echoed throughout the room. An elderly priest had collapsed face-first onto the table.

"Father!"

The chamberlains gathered around him and carried him out. The door to the office opened, and like the collapse of a dam blocking a river's flow, the tension washed away.

The archbishop watched this turn of events and raised his eyes from the parchment, then spoke.

"We cannot hold a meeting like this. I have not finished reading this translation, so let us reconvene tomorrow."

It was not only the priests who felt relieved. Hyland's attendants, including Col, exhaled the breaths they had been holding.

But then—

"The night is long, so I will wait until you finish," Hyland declared resolutely. The archbishop's expression tensed, and his words caught in his throat. His fellow priests, almost instinctively, looked to him for guidance.

Admiration overwhelmed Col. Hyland was most certainly no fanciful noble.

He had been waiting this entire time for his opponent's tension to ease.

Hyland stared at the archbishop, as though declaring his intention to follow through all the way to hell, unwilling to back off. Realizing this, the archbishop was dumbstruck.

However, the priests under him had showed they were at their limit, both physically and mentally. More than anything, they had relaxed for a moment in relief that the day was over. It was virtually impossible for them to gather themselves once again. The tables had turned.

It was possible that the archbishop had underestimated Hyland. After all, he was a weak noble, brought up in a manor. His delicate features even made him look feminine, and there was certainly nothing crude about him. But he had the perseverance that a hunter could appreciate, as well as a hint of mischief about him like a merchant outwitting an opponent.

"Urgh…Guh…"

The archbishop broke into a heavy sweat and groaned, but he was also a man who deserved his place in a seat of power.

"Yes…Indeed. We mustn't leave this unfinished."

He fixed Hyland with a biting gaze, not to be outdone. Perhaps this was the look of one pulling another into the grave with them. The priests' expressions were all hopeless, but they did not go against the archbishop's word.

Then, after carefully considering the situation, Hyland spoke.

"But first, why don't we have a bite to eat?"

Col thought for a moment that this would just refresh their opponents, but when he saw the expressions on their faces, he understood.

Their feelings were clearly leaning in favor of Hyland. They would see him as a savior.

The archbishop, realizing he had been beaten to the punch, nodded painfully.

"Urgh…Then, bring us bread and drink. The stalls should still be open in town."

The chamberlains bowed their heads, and they all left the office. Hyland turned back toward Col and spoke with a refreshing smile.

"You go and help them, too."

It was clear that he was not treating them as servants, but offering a chance to stretch and get some relief, disguised as a command.

However, in this battle of stamina, his guards refused to part with him and answered, "With all due respect." Should their master endure pain, then they would do the same.

"Then, the rest of you, prepare the meals."

They had been standing in the same place all day, so Col felt like his knees and back were no longer his.

Myuri faltered as well, and Col supported her slim frame.

"Are you all right?"

"…I want to take a bath."

"Me, too," he responded lightly with a smile. Outside of the office, everyone was bending their knees and stretching. There were no friends or enemies in these shared actions. Though there was a hint of sourness between the chamberlains and Hyland's attendants, they all shared sympathy for each other.

That being said, it seemed they preferred not to be seen going to the market together, so the chamberlains took the back entrance while Hyland's attendants used the front gates. Col and Myuri had to buy food for themselves as well, but Myuri's legs seemed like they hurt, so they decided to rest in the corner of a hallway along the way.

"That was awful."

Myuri sat on a stack of crates along the side of the passageway and spoke with a smile.

"That blondie really has a nasty personality."

Col unwittingly looked around, but no one was there. The assistant priests who were busily running around inside the church were probably in the main hall for evening prayers. And he detected a kind of respect in her words.

It was as if she was impressed.

"If you were sitting there, Brother, you would have given up before that old man got to the third page."

And never mind all the subordinate priests' emotions resting on his shoulders. It was impossible and out of the question.

"But what are those guys planning?" she mused.

He was less concerned about her acerbic manner of speech than about who exactly she was referring to.

""Those guys'?"

"Blondie and the old man. They both have a chance of winning, after all."

"I thought about that, too."

Hyland was waiting for the people to grow angry while the archbishop was waiting for the people to lose interest in the fight.

When he informed her of this, Myuri was extremely exasperated.

"See, Brother, that's why you're no good."

"N-no good, why?"

Myuri raised her foot onto the crate and rested her chin on her knee. She looked like the boss of a children's gang, about to lay out her plan to beat up the kids in the next village over.

"You're good at archery and you're stubborn, so walking

around and hunting deer with a bow and arrow suits you. But you're bad at hunting for numbers and traps."

He did not know what she was talking about all of a sudden, but it was true. He would sometimes take his bow and arrow out into the mountains and shoot deer. His hunter acquaintances would applaud his results. However, when Myuri hunted in the mountains, they would grow heated, calling it an infringement on their territory. That was because she could catch enough squirrels and rabbits to live off any profits from their furs.

"Hunting with traps tests how nasty you are."

"...Nasty?"

"You make lots of traps, then you create a path that forces and chases prey into it."

Myuri was brilliant with such things, and Col himself was not. He knew nothing of the routes of squirrels and how the rabbits returned to their holes. He had a hard time efficiently looking at the big picture.

"It's because you're kind and honest."

Myuri smiled.

"And that blondie must be plotting something because it's obvious that old man has no one to turn to. The yelling strategy caught that man off guard yesterday, remember? That's the makings of a hunter there. There's no way that happened randomly without any preparation."

"And so?" he asked, and Myuri shrugged.

"That blondie knows that it'll take something more fundamental than a cheap resolution to turn the tide and make the old man give up. If not today, then tomorrow."

Just then, his memory jumped to that dark night.

"No...way."

Maybe that commotion, that boiling malice had not happened naturally.

To think that Hyland would do such a thing—that he would devalue the Church's authority.

Col was at a loss for words from the shock, while Myuri merely looked on sadly.

"No matter how kind you are to the world, it doesn't mean the world has to be kind to you."

She appeared the same as she did when he was braiding her hair in front of the world map.

At that time, she was trying to hide her beast's ears, her tail, and that she was a girl. No matter how curious she was about the outside world, the world would surely treat her cruelly.

Myuri had already realized that many years ago when she was very little.

"Blondie knows that in a few days, the town will be in a riot, which explains the confidence. But then, Brother."

Myuri was gazing straight at him.

"That would be weird."

"Weird? What could be more than...?"

"You remember, too, don't you? It's easy to make someone angry, but much harder to calm them down."

Myuri suddenly grinned mischievously, and Col in turn smiled weakly. He remembered how much trouble it had been in the past to handle Myuri something had set her off.

"That's...true."

"But I don't think that old man has no plan, though. He has to have something up his sleeve, too. But I have no idea what it might be. Your plan is too easygoing. It's like fishing without a lure and just hoping some fish will bite it by accident. That's why he must have some sort of strategy to deal with the crazy townspeople."

Once she mentioned it, that sounded possible.

Both the archbishop and Hyland had large burdens to bear. There was no way either of them would wait placidly. He did not want to imagine that Hyland had deliberately conspired to create such a dark atmosphere in town for such purposes, but it made sense logically. Then what about the archbishop? What was he waiting for?

"If we can figure out the archbishop's plan, then we will be able to help Heir Hyland..."

"Well, what we do know is that it's not something you'll be able to figure out."

He shot her a frown, and she replied, "That just means you're a nice person." It did not cheer him up. After teasing him like that for a while, Myuri stood up from the crate, the weariness in her legs now gone, and held his hand.

"I'm hungry."

"All right, all right."

They then retrieved their meals from the square, and since both their food and breath seemed liable to catch in their throats if they ate in the office, they quickly took their meals at the side of the church. It was too early to call it nightfall, but the sky had turned cinnabar red, and the languid comfort that came from finishing work settled over the town. The more impatient stalls were already beginning to close down, and bars began lighting the candles in stands outside their shops, preparing braziers and tables.

However, once the sun set, the atmosphere in town would change dramatically. Once the warm, lively, and bright daytime fell away, the cold, chaotic, torch-lit night would come.

It did not seem that Hyland would leave once evening arrived, so at night the fight would really begin.

"Are you finished eating?"

Myuri nodded as she licked the pad of her thumb.

"I do not mind if you slip out if you start to feel unwell," he reminded her, and Myuri cheekily shrugged her slim shoulders.

"And be sure not to collapse when someone is mean to you, Brother."

With an attitude like that, she would be fine.

Then, they returned to the church once again, for the sake of God's correct teachings.

When they returned to the office, the atmosphere had mellowed, most likely due to the meal break. The elderly priest who collapsed earlier still seemed pale but was sitting in his seat. Most of the priests' chamberlains were present, and Col and Myuri were a bit flustered when they entered the room. They could tell they were among the last.

However, when Col noticed the archbishop turning the pages of the parchment, reading the rest, he was blown away. What sort of change of heart was this?

He could not imagine that the archbishop had been so enthralled by the teachings of the scripture that he could not stop reading. More plausible was that he was planning to move on to the next step in order to prevent the priests, who were his underlings and companions, from feeling even more alienated by the test of endurance.

The question was what that plan was.

Hyland's strategy involved using the demeanor of the townspeople. He did not want to think that he was directly agitating them himself, like Myuri had said, but he had enough incentive to do so. Once night fell, the archbishop was the one who would have to concede in the face of the atmosphere created by the people abusing the name of the Church in the square.

Then what was the archbishop after?

In any case, there was no mistaking that everyone here was trying to outsmart the other. What were the angels thinking as they gazed down at them from the walls? Perhaps they thought it was too late for much of anything.

As Col pondered this, the chamberlains on the priests' side looked around the room, counting everyone present before closing the door that led into the office. It was like placing a lid on the room to ensure the miasma would not seep outside.

Everything fell silent once again, and the archbishop continued reading. He was not simply moving his eyes along the page, but was obviously reading it carefully. As one of the translators, Col was simply nervous. What part was he reading now? What did he think of the quality of the translation? Was anything that he learned useful in the real world?

Col understood that ambition was not easily quenched.

Then, he finally felt he appreciated a small fragment of the archbishops' feelings as they desperately clung to the privilege within this magnificent cathedral, no matter what others said, and no matter how far they strayed from the teachings of God.

It was unlikely that Col's thoughts had reached the elderly clergyman, but the archbishop's eyes suddenly paused at one part of the parchment. He reread the previous line, as though something had caught his interest, and read it over again.

It was clear from how he showed it to the priest next to him that it was not simply a way of wasting time. That priest looked at the indication section, and his eyes widened. He then showed it to the priest next to him.

Col desperately wanted to know which part they were talking about and why.

Judging by its place in the stack of parchment, there was no doubting that it was a part that he translated.

He stood on his toes and leaned forward, trying to take a peek, to get just a hint of which part they were passing around. The moment he saw the contents of the parchment as it slid onto the table, a chill ran down his spine. It was clearly his writing. He gulped, knowing that those with status and power were reading the words he had written.

Consumed by an inexplicable excitement, Col found his feet subconsciously moved forward. Myuri pulled on his clothes and stepped on his toes, and Hyland was smiling faintly at him over his shoulder.

He felt like he was the only child in the room.

The parchment circulated as this was happening and made its way back to the archbishop.

The archbishop placed it carefully on top of another pile of parchment and cleared his throat.

"I am surprised that this is the common-language translation of the scripture that the world is seeing."

Everyone in that room understood that it was not simply an opinion.

Hyland responded politely. "We wish for at least some of the people of the world to know of God's teachings. I'm sure you've understood that it is not something meant to rile up the people."

The archbishop nodded slowly at his answer.

"I hope you do not mind me asking, but who was the one who translated this? A famous theologian of the Winfiel Kingdom, perhaps?"

At that moment, he sensed that Myuri's hair, which was simply tied back, was bristling like the fur on her tail did sometimes. There was no doubting that the handwriting on the parchment that had slid across the table was Col's. That part was his.

"No, the young scholar here was the one who worked on the part you are holding now."

Hyland introduced him, and Col stretched his back as high as he could and raised his gaze. By no means could he take in all the priests' gazes. He instead turned toward the crest of the Church that hung on the wall in front of him. It was as though God was blessing him for all that he had learned by granting it some small meaning, here in this great house meant for spreading his teachings.

"I see. And you were the one who asked this young scholar to do the translation?"

"Indeed. We in the Kingdom of Winfiel do not wish to keep the teachings of God to ourselves, and certainly God wishes for the same."

That was the first strike, but the archbishop simply let it pass.

"Mm. Well, if this is the result of Heir Hyland, and by extent, the Kingdom of Winfiel's careful consideration, then there is nothing to be done."

The archbishop sounded impressed, but Col could not understand the meaning of his words.

He could just barely see Hyland's expression ahead of him, and he was keeping his composure, so perhaps Hyland was supposed to understand, as well.

As he considered this, a grave question came from the archbishop's mouth.

"Very well, may I consider what is written here the responsibility of Heir Hyland and of the Kingdom of Winfiel?"

Something was odd about the situation.

Hyland seemed flustered because the archbishop's actions were going further than expected.

There was only one reason for him to say such a thing after passing around the parchment. There was plenty of room for debate, because to translate the words and phrases of the scripture was to give it particular meaning. However, by Hyland's judgment, the archbishop of Atiph had probably never thoroughly read it. Could it be that he was going to quiz them on matters of God's teachings, after all?

He wondered if there were obvious mistakes, but he corrected himself—no. He had looked it over countless times. And there should be no place that could be easily attacked.

One of the chamberlains brought the parchment to Hyland. From this close distance, he could tell that the familiar writing was his, and it was a part where the prophet's words were praising God. There was nothing here that could be open to interpretation or a metaphor.

Hyland, too, seemed to be able to tell exactly which part of the translation it was at a glance and handed it to Col without reading anything in particular.

"Is there something wrong with this?"

He received the parchment from him and began reading the beginning of each line. There were no mistakes, as he expected. As he read his own writing, he recalled his excitement and happiness and his battle with sleepiness in the middle of the night and the pain in his back as he wrote it.

But Myuri pulled on his clothes.

She approached the document looking not at the letters but the parchment itself.

"This…"

She began to speak, but the archbishop spoke at roughly the same time.

"The line fourth from the bottom—is it not a moving passage in the original scripture that repeats praises to God many times?"

Fourth from the bottom?

He began reading backward.

Then, he unwittingly raised his voice.

"What?"

He could feel Hyland turn around, but that was not what bothered him at the moment. He could not believe his eyes. His balance faltered, and he felt bile rising in his throat.

What was this?

"Col, what's wrong?"

He could not even move his eyes. Hyland stood from his chair and snatched the parchment from him. He then immediately flinched and looked up. The man who had spent the entire day unfazed by the soul-crushing test of endurance was now reeling from head to toe.

But he looked not at Col—but at the archbishop.

"No…What? How…?"

That word saved him. Indeed—how?

It was impossible that was his own mistake. The passage that should have been singing praises of God described him as a pig, and all his wisdom was replaced with nothing but pig noises.

"There is no cause for shock; the writing is all the same. There is no mistaking that young scholar wrote these words under your patronage."

At the archbishop's words, Hyland looked down with a pained expression at the parchment in his hand. The writing did indeed match.

It was so perfectly, so eerily Col's handwriting.

He could only imagine that a demon snuck in during the night and wrote those things at its leisure.

Then—

"Brother, it smells like the scribes."

When Myuri whispered to him, Col understood everything.

He had asked three scribes to do the copies. One of them could not read. However, that actually meant he was a skilled scribe.

Why? Because letters were just like pictures on a certain level, and copying them perfectly was a job well done.

Then, with the ability to reproduce any writing, they could forge anything by simply rearranging words. A wolf could hide in plain sight under sheep's skin. Someone had snuck into Col and Myuri's room. It had all been planned. Myuri's warning was correct.

Col regretted deeply that he had not checked more carefully, but it was too late.

"The only ones you should blame are those who would use such underhanded tricks, Col."

It was at that moment Hyland called out to him. Their eyes met, and the young man nodded.

"And someone may have switched them while we were not watching during the break. We were not cautious enough."

If the parchment had been switched the day before, there was certainly a higher risk of being discovered. In that light, Hyland's proposition seemed the most likely.

Pain still remained in Col's chest, but Hyland had helped to relieve his unease and let him think more clearly. At any rate, this was not a time to blame himself.

Though it was fact that they had been tricked, Col wondered if there was any meaning to such an obvious ruse. Clearly, since forgery was well within the realm of possibility, it would be fruitless to argue whether he had really written it or not. Most of all, the offending sentence was so blatantly intentional that it seemed excessive.

Was this the archbishop's way of stalling for even more time? But what would happen if word got out that they butted heads over such a thing? Rather than accept that Hyland and his subordinates like Col had gone insane, it seemed more likely for the townspeople to assume the archbishop had carried out some dishonorable scheme.

He could only imagine it would have the complete opposite effect of what the archbishop wanted.

Supposing it did cause something to happen, that would be...

When he hit upon the answer, the blood drained from his face.

"Those who have written such a passage..." The archbishop raised his voice. "...Are apt to be called heretics, are they not?"

"What?!"

When Hyland yelled, the doors to the office burst open.

There stood the town's garrison, lined up in formation.

"Cease all resistance! You are suspected for the creation, possession, and circulation of banned heretical literature!"

"Impossible!"

As though Hyland's exclamation was a signal, his guards placed their hands on the sheaths of their swords. They did not draw because doing so in a sacred house would immediately make them traitors.

Suspicion of heresy.

Now Col could see what the archbishop was doing, but there was something he still did not understand. Members of the city's garrison should have been unable to act without the city council's command. The council of a free city such as Atiph was comprised of local nobles and important merchants. Did they not already show support for Hyland's plight?

If he had not misunderstood, then there must have been one last missing piece to this puzzle.

Then, the key to everything suddenly appeared before the soldiers.

"Y-you're..."

Hyland gulped, and Col doubted his own eyes as well. The

priests and archbishop all stood from their seats and placed their hands against their chests in a gesture of respect for God. A lone man who was on the older end of middle age appeared from among the guards, wearing pure white robes. Painted on his vestments was the crest of the Church in a bright crimson. The one who wore these robes was granted the protection and safe passage of any ruler or power holder, free from all regulation.

That was because there was only one thing that reigned over this man, and it was the word of God.

And that was because he traveled the world, entrusted with all the authority of God's earthly proxy that was the pope—this man was a papal officer.

"I hereby announce in the name of the pope—"

He spoke in a heavy, distinct voice that did not allow for idle chatter as he produced a single piece of parchment.

"We recognize the ideas put forth by the Kingdom of Winfiel as heresy, and all literature not dictated by God himself banned. The one hundred and seventeenth pope, Einmel Desir the Seventeenth."

From far away, Col could not tell if the wax seal on the parchment was real or not.

However, if the papal officer had falsified the official sanction, then the target of the inquisition's examination would be the archbishop.

It had to be genuine.

"All under Hyland are arrested in the name of God."

Soldiers poured into the room. Hyland's guards lowered themselves in order to strike back, but he stopped them with a wave of his hand. There was no other choice. They were outnumbered, and if it came to pass that they lost after daring to draw their swords, there was no telling what sort of dishonor would stain his reputation. Blood was truly the most eloquent storyteller.

And as the soldiers drew closer, rope in hand, Hyland quickly judged their expressions. On an emotional level, they were still on his side, though they had no choice but to act when the papal officer showed up.

There remained a chance to turn the tide.

For that, they had to remain innocent.

"God favors the righteous."

They were arrested, and as they were being led out of the office, Hyland spoke those words to the archbishop. The archbishop averted his eyes with a tense expression, then suddenly showed the papal officer a flattering smile.

Col and Myuri were also ushered away by the soldiers through the back entrance where everyone was squeezed into wagons.

They were not escorted through the front due to the possibility of igniting the townspeople's anger if they were seen.

Then the wagons traveled for quite a while even though the town was small. The soldiers, who did not bother to hide their sympathy, had placed Col and Myuri in the same wagon, perhaps because she clung to him the entire time. He wanted to hold her hand, but he could not because his hands were tied behind his back.

The wagon rattled along. Col could tell that the ground had changed from paved stone to a hard dirt path at some point. When everyone finally stepped out, they were surrounded by what seemed to be fields and orchards.

"Is this…outside of town?" Myuri asked Col quietly. Only one thing came to mind when he imagined prisoners being taken to a place devoid of people. What was more, the earth was perfectly plowed.

However, as he looked around, restraining his pounding heart, he could see the city walls beyond the trees. Certainly, they would not be suddenly put to death within the city.

"Come."

The soldiers pulled the rope, bringing them around the wagon, and he was finally relieved.

They had arrived at a large manor, which was not uncommon to see in rural areas and was most likely owned by the city nobles.

CHAPTER FOUR

"There will be further orders. Stay put."

They entered the manor. Hyland's guards were led underground, and then Hyland himself and his remaining entourage, including Col and Myuri, were brought upstairs. Their party was divided again as they walked down the halls, but luckily, Col was placed in the same room as Myuri. He was unsure if it was intentional, but Myuri had been calling him "Brother" loud enough for the soldiers to hear. That was probably why.

At any rate, the cautionary rope restraints were removed from their wrists, and they were pushed into a room that resembled the lodging at a simple inn. There were no decorations—just a bed, desk, and chair. It was clearly anticlimactic for Myuri. Perhaps she imagined they would be put into a leaky, rat-infested, stone dungeon.

"It seems like they're treating us as people of a certain standing."

Col rubbed his now unbound wrists and opened the window, where he discovered a grid of metal bars, similar to the ones commonly found on prison cells. In the distance, he could see tall buildings and the church's bell tower. It all seemed so far away, not because the sun had set and it was difficult to judge distance in the darkness, but because he was mentally exhausted. He tried to imagine the townspeople rising up and flooding the church to save them after learning about the arrest, but Col did not have it in him.

He tried to shake the bars in the window, but they did not so much as wiggle. The entrance, too, was unusual. The door was a wood lattice fixed with sturdy metal hinges. Maybe it was a measure to prevent surprise attacks on anyone opening the door from the outside, allowing visual confirmation that the prisoners inside were not planning anything suspicious.

He looked at the wall to see if there were any openings and noticed that words had been scribbled all over the surface. "Glory to our banner!" "O spirits of great heroes, praise your justice," "Shoulda killed that bastard subordinate when I had the chance"—they were the scrawling of the fairly influential people thrown in here long ago.

"Those scribes were traitors," Myuri said while she rubbed her wrists.

"I'm sorry I didn't heed your warnings."

"I told you so…is what I want to say, but what blondie said was true. There's nothing we can do."

It just so happened that Col had been targeted.

"But what are we going to do now, Brother?" she asked in a lowered voice, sounding anxious but somehow theatrical at the same time. Perhaps Myuri was recalling the smattering of adventure stories she had heard so many times.

"Though the pope has sanctioned us as heretics, I do not think we will be beheaded immediately. I think inquisitors will hold an examination first."

"Oh, I know about that. That's when they burn witches at the stake, right?"

She must have heard that from a guest at the bathhouse.

"They won't do anything barbaric that would start widespread rumors. Especially since Heir Hyland is here."

Before their conversation, after calmly thinking about it, Col still could not really believe the pope's sanction. The designation of "heretic" normally had the impression of something grander, a compelling force that could ravage entire regions, unbending in the face of the Church's negotiations and persuasions, fueling outrage until it was finally exhausted. Looking back on history, the recognition and subjugation of heresy was often used as an excuse to suppress revolting peasants. In that respect, many lords must have been carefully watching the development of this commotion, especially since the Kingdom of Winfiel and the pope had been negotiating for three years already. Any rash moves were just as likely to come back and haunt the pope.

Hyland had come to the town of Atiph as a representative of the kingdom, so to deem him a heretic and arrest him was hardly any different from a declaration of war on the Kingdom of Winfiel.

Therefore, Col could not discount the possibility that it was actually a terrifyingly dangerous farce planned by the archbishop.

"But at any rate, if we don't resolve this situation and if the papal officer was genuine, then Heir Hyland's plans will go to dust. Oh God…"

Col paced around the room, wondering if there was anything they could do; Myuri spoke up from her spot on the bed, exasperated.

"Brother, shouldn't we worry about ourselves before other people?"

"Of course, but…"

"Then, how are we going to get out? Under the cover of night? Or knocking out all the guards?"

Had Myuri's ears and tail been out, they would have been twitching in excitement. Though it might have also been a sign of her anxiety, it was more likely that she was busy mixing reality and fiction after having read too many adventure stories when they lived at the bathhouse.

On the other hand, it was true that they had to do something. The most trustworthy connection they could rely on at the moment was their relationship with the Debau Company. As Col thought about how to get a hold of them, he could hear the sound of a latticed door opening somewhere in the connecting hallway. The echoes of many footsteps drew closer. Perhaps they were bringing someone out from another room.

Col held his breath and looked out onto the hallway, where he saw Hyland surrounded on all sides by soldiers. His hands were still tied in front of him, and the sight was painful.

"Mm? Oh, wait a second."

Hyland noticed the two of them and called out to the guards.

Then, they all stopped, feigning ignorance as they stepped back.

"We have lots of allies. It's too early to give up."

He smiled at them through the lattice. But that smile quickly disappeared.

"Sorry for getting you swept up in all this."

"Not at all. But what is going on? I cannot bring myself to believe this accusation of heresy is real. Is this all a show planned by the archbishop?"

"I want to believe that, too, but according to the soldiers, it's real. A boat arrived at the port just before we took our break, and the city council was gathered at a moment's notice. And what we heard was the resulting judgment. The archbishop probably knew beforehand that the papal officer was on the way with the sanction. That was why he was wasting so much time."

"B-but arresting you means that the pope…"

"I realized that as well. It looks like he's planning to go to war with my country. Next, I will likely be interrogated to reveal all the allies I've recruited here on the mainland."

Col stared blankly in response, and Hyland closed his eyes. Rather than being afraid of torture, it seemed like he was struggling with shame, enduring the torments of his conscience—or so Col imagined.

"There's something I didn't tell you."

When Hyland finished speaking, he looked straight at Col. Perhaps it was dignity as a noble or perhaps just his personality.

"Our ultimate goal is to create a new church."

For the briefest of moments, Col could not believe it. The Kingdom of Winfiel had been lacking proper religious activity for three years. How many people had been praying for God's intercession during that time?

Then, after hearing just that one sentence, Col understood the reason for the severity of the pope's response. If he and the rest of the Church allowed a country as large as the Kingdom of Winfiel to create its own church, then it was not difficult to imagine that others would soon follow suit.

For the pope, there was no other choice but to strike first.

"That was somehow leaked to the pope. But luckily for us, he struck the first blow, so we now have an excellent reason to fight back."

After Hyland spoke, he slowly dropped to one knee, bowing his head.

"I am sincerely sorry for not telling you about this. But I had expected we would not be making it public for a while. The pope dispatched a number of cardinals who are currently in the kingdom. I did not think that he would make his move while they were still there. Or perhaps he took advantage of the moment while we had our guard down…"

Like a spider, the plan had scuttled around and caught them in its web.

"And since we did not know how much you agreed with our ideas, I couldn't tell you. I can do nothing but extend my apologies for how it ended up seeming like we deceived you."

The bathhouse master and former merchant Lawrence would say that it cost nothing to bow humbly and that doing so as much as possible was the pride of a merchant. Hyland, however, came from the blood of royalty. It was no small thing for such a person to lower his head.

"Heir Hyland, please stop. I am aware, to an extent, how dangerous it is. But we must think of a way to get out of this situation."

Hyland still kept his head down and finally raised it after a while. "I have a request to ask of you in regards to that."

"A request?"

"Yes. But it is something our young miss will most certainly not fancy this time."

Col looked away from Hyland's tired smile, and Myuri was glaring at him with such ferocity. It was the same glare she gave to the girl that invited him into that inn.

Myuri was consistent in her distrust of Hyland. She was convinced the noble was hiding something.

That ended up being true, but when Col considered Hyland's position, he understood why Hyland had acted that way. In the end, Col was nothing but a working boy in the baths of Nyohhira. He was not someone who could be easily trusted with secrets.

"There is something I must confirm beforehand. The story I told you in Nyohhira has already changed. What we do next will not be something that the pope simply does not care for. To cooperate with me is to join with the Kingdom of Winfiel. You understand what that means, correct?"

They would no longer be mere critics of the pope's actions but directly opposing the pope's authority itself.

The pope was the voice of God on earth, and the Church that he ruled over was an institution meant to spread and teach the fundamentals of righteousness to the people of the world. Within that organization, contradictions, corruption, and abuse were rampant. And yet people still frequently went to church, offered donations, and respected their priests. That had continued uninterrupted for over a thousand years.

Such an unbending world continued to expand, and the past decades bore witness to bloody conflict with the pagans in the northlands. Though the fight petered out indecisively, the war cooled down in a way that could be considered a victory for the Church.

During that period, a number of countries were destroyed, and rulers had been driven from their lands.

The Kingdom of Winfiel wanted to battle against such a gigantic organization.

"It will be dangerous, and probably a long, intense fight. But I want you to imagine."

"Ima...gine...?"

"Yes. With our own hands, we can create a new church—a church where the presiding priests teach from a scripture translated into the common language for all to read. Injustice and abuse will largely decrease. We can sweep away the things that we pretended not to see and things we could do nothing about. That is why I did not call on the high-ranking clergy at the bathhouse, sitting in the baths like overly boiled turnips, but you. We want to create a new world. A world without deception or lies."

Other people would question if that was actually possible.

However, what those people should have done was read the scripture. The original prophets of their religion had thrived in pagan lands filled with even more widespread and twisted teachings than what the current Church represented.

"And it is not just an ideal. We have a fair chance of winning this fight."

Hyland glanced up and down the hall, then drew closer to the latticed door and lowered his voice even more.

"Our kingdom is an island. It is not easy to send a large army even to the northlands, which is on the mainland. More importantly, we have plentiful fishing grounds and shipbuilding skills. The pope played his hand so quickly because he was afraid we would manage to complete our preparations."

Just by looking at the number of fish brought to Atiph's port town, Col understood what that meant. The fish caught in the northern seas reached dinner tables far inland, and there was still much left over. Hyland was saying they were not cornered in a fight where they had no chance of winning, and those words were persuasive.

All the conditions had been met.

The only thing left to do was stand up.

"Col, I want your skills," Hyland said.

"After, I will most absolutely repay you. There should be more than enough room to find a seat for you in the new Church."

Hyland meant they would accommodate Col during the creation of the new Church. The young man could not even force himself to say that he did not want that. To stand in the pastoral cornerstone would mean being able to deliver salvation to many people.

But talk about the new Church that Hyland and the Kingdom of Winfiel would create was much more enthralling than that. If it were to come to fruition, then a great deal of the masses would become able to receive the true teachings of God.

However, there was still one thing that bothered him.

"Heir Hyland, I want to ask you something."

"What is it?"

This kind of question was, in a sense, betraying Hyland.

However, it was not that simple to change a point of view of something that had continued for so long.

"Is the purpose of this new Church to overthrow the existing Church?"

While there were bad aspects to the Church, there were also some good. Col's wish was not to smash it into millions of pieces but to straighten the warped pillars.

"I don't want to do that. If we create a new church, this Church may change their ideas. As it stands, I think it may stay the way it is now for all of eternity."

It was not anger that brimmed in Hyland's eyes.

What crossed his mind was the archbishop's humble smile as he flattered the papal officer.

The world would not change so easily.

"Of course, I hope a world will come where, as a result of this change, the people have the choice of choosing whichever church they fancy—new or old."

"...It sounds like you're supposing such a thing could never be a reality."

"It is not wholly a problem of faith. This is politics. We must do everything in our power to make sure it does not end up that way. Someone must take the step forward."

Hyland's gaze was piercing.

There would be danger.

But Col once left his village without paying a single mind to that danger.

Then he remembered the moment he had felt that some things in this world were worth believing in.

"What can I do?"

It was immediately after he said that.

"No."

Myuri, who had been listening beside him the whole time, interrupted.

Then, she pushed herself between him and Hyland, forcing him back farther into the room.

"No, he won't do it. Brother's not gonna help the likes of you."

"M-Myuri?!"

Col managed to straighten his posture and hold her back.

He sensed her strength—she was sincere.

"That's enough…"

"No, you should listen to what the little miss has to say."

For a moment, Col did not know who spoke. On the other side of Myuri, Hyland was smiling.

"I don't want to trick or threaten people to join my side. I've had too much of the taste of that in the court."

His smile was so soft, Col almost thought it belonged to a woman, but his eyes were cold as glass.

"I have had so many brothers who did not share my blood. But the kind ones who stood by me or paid attention to the feelings of others either perished or were sent away. The ones who remain are the cockroaches that refuse to die."

He had heard that bloody fights between those of the same flesh and blood were endless in the circles of nobility. He imagined that those quarrels became incomparable once rights of succession were included in the equation. Once he understood that from Hyland's perspective, he felt it was clear why Hyland himself possessed an impressive amount of theological knowledge. It was impossible all that was gained hastily for show. He needed it to heal the hunger and scars of his soul.

And perhaps that was the reason he always gave candy and kind words to the ill-mannered Myuri.

"I have my own reasons to look to God for guidance, much like how you want to stop your brother."

"..."

Myuri stopped and fell into a frozen silence. Did Hyland know why she was acting up?

Then the noble looked toward the hallway and must have realized that it was time. He stood and spoke quickly.

"Col, the Debau Company should be coming for you two. When they do, ask them to think of a way to save me. At this rate, I will just be used as a hostage of war. The Kingdom of Winfiel will already be at a disadvantage, and without me, wicked plans might worm their way into the creation of the new Church."

However, Hyland was of royal blood, and people with such power should have many avenues to seek assistance.

It was just as Col was wondering why the Debau Company would come save them and not Hyland.

"The Debau Company will not come to my rescue unconditionally. They will be weighing the scales of profit."

Hyland and the Debau Company were tied together by mutual gain. Once things began going well for the kingdom in their fight against the pope, the Debau Company would obtain trade privileges. That was why the company cooperated and accommodated him. It was simply for personal gain. There had to be something that was of equal value to rescuing Hyland, who had been declared a heretic by the pope and arrested on orders of the city council.

"Th-then, we'll call on the kingdom—"

Col was about to argue, but Hyland stopped him with a kind smile.

"My family is even more untrustworthy. If I did rely on them, there's no small chance they would assassinate me."

Col was shocked.

"If they went as far as negotiating with the pope over a hostage, that is to say myself, then they would likely arrange for me to become the first martyr of our new Church. They could remove an enemy from the court while also cultivating the people's support. They would rejoice at the opportunity to kill two birds with one stone. That is why I had no choice but to pin my hopes on you two. You have deep connections with the Debau Company, beyond anything that could be weighed for profit."

That moment, Col finally realized the biggest reason why he was the one that Hyland brought from Nyohhira.

Hyland was connected to the Debau by profit, but Col and Myuri were different. They were family of the so-called powerhouses behind the scenes of the company, and they were treated as such. That was why Hyland so calmly calculated in Nyohhira that whatever happened, they would be rescued without any considerations to potential gain. In addition, he planned that when danger came for himself, he would borrow that influence.

Col felt no need to despise such calculation. He was not discouraged that they had been used, either.

That was because Hyland wore such a pained expression on his face. He even seemed regretful.

Hyland had said he could not depend on his family. In this seaside town, where he could faintly see the Kingdom of Winfiel on a clear day from the top of the church bell tower, he was fighting for his homeland.

Hyland, no longer having anything else to say, stood as though he had resigned himself to his fate. He walked off before Col could say anything, and the soldiers hurriedly followed.

Col's mind was so packed with innumerable thoughts, he felt his head might burst. Before him was a stack of problems he could not have even imagined back in Nyohhira. To be honest, he did not even know where to begin.

But more than ten years ago, he stood by the side of a merchant who had boldly faced each and every hardship.

What would Lawrence do?

No matter what, he should begin with the problems right in front of him.

"Myuri."

Hyland had seen through her somehow, and at the moment she was silent, as though a spell had been cast on her. Just like how Hyland had concealed certain things, Myuri was hiding something, too.

He called her name, and she suddenly came back to reality before drawing away from him. Perhaps she was surprised, as her back hit the latticed door before she sank to the floor with a *thud*.

Col was about to rush to her side when she stopped him with her gaze.

Had it been hostile and piercing, he would have been able to face it.

But instead, Myuri seemed like she was about to cry.

"A-are we going to…save that blondie?"

He thought for a moment that she was simply using tears to get her way, as she had done many times in the past. That being said, he had been with her since the moment he heard her cries at birth. He could always tell how serious she was.

His head hurt because her tears were genuine.

"Myuri."

He called her name again, and he sat on the floor with a sigh. It had been quite a while since he last stooped to Myuri's eye level. He had often lectured her like this long ago when she would not listen to him.

"I can't do anything about how tomboyish you are, but you received your intellect from Holo. You are also perceptive. And I know that you are truly kind. Are you saying you don't want to save Heir Hyland, even after learning about his position? Or do you think everything we heard just now is a lie?"

Her usual competitive spirit had quieted, and she was at a loss. It looked like she might begin crying with one more push, as her hair bristled while she squirmed.

"Myuri, your ears."

She hurriedly pressed down on her head and curled up, keeping her hands there. She tightened herself into a ball like she wanted to hide in a place where no one would find her. He understood that she must have a good reason for doing so, but he could not imagine what.

However, she did not answer when he asked, and he was used to dealing with troublesome beings who would not give a reason for avoiding his questions. What was more, unlike an elusive God, Myuri was most definitely in front of him.

"You've had this attitude ever since Heir Hyland came to the bathhouse."

Myuri continued to curl inward, as though being beaten with a stick.

"At first, I thought you were simply sulking because I was busy dealing with him."

He could not see her face anymore.

"You've kept acting this way even until now, which means that this isn't a whim of yours."

Like a root, hidden deep under the ground, something was there.

"Is it something that makes it okay to treat troubled people and their important goals so cruelly?"

Then, as he watched her, he could clearly tell that Myuri herself was lost and in pain. Even still, she did not want him to help Hyland.

Col truly did not want to use this method because he was dealing with Myuri, but it was his last resort.

"Why do you wish to get in the way of my dreams?"

From the gap between her arms cradling her head, her expression pierced him.

She widened her eyes, her whole body tensed like cornered prey, and she tightened her lips. Her body shrank in on itself enough she seemed about to disappear, and her last line of defense crumbled.

Then, what appeared were eyes brimming with anger.

"If you...if you want to know so bad, I'll tell you...Okay?"

Col had not expected she would fight back, so he recoiled. Her arms had just been holding her head as if to protect herself, but now they appeared to be suppressing something that might explode.

He had been sure she would defend herself and give her reasons as she cried. Then, he had imagined how he would gently listen to her and quietly admonish her. He had not thought she would defiantly bully him.

As he kept still for reasons even he did not know, Myuri declared again, "It will definitely, *definitely* upset you, but fine."

Was this Myuri's oddly intelligent strategy? Was she planning to bare her fangs and hope he retreated?

Col stood in an awkward position, and there was now something that would trouble him even more. Hyland had been taken hostage, the pope had banned the translation of the scripture, plus he and Myuri were in jail at the moment. If things continued like this, the teachings of God would remain warped, and it was even doubtful if they would live long enough to return to Nyohhira.

But Myuri, who stood face-to-face with him, did not seem to be lying. He trusted her. She lowered her arms from around her head and let out a great sigh that even reached her shoulders as she stared unwaveringly at him. It was a glare full of anger that blamed him for everything.

A silence similar to the one he had just experienced in the office overcame them.

Myuri was the one who tore it apart with her fangs.

"I don't want to make trouble for you."

She had to speak slowly, and he listened carefully as he did not know what would come out of her mouth next. That was how stiffly she spoke.

"But even I...have some things I don't want to give up."

Typically, the word *modest* did not apply to Myuri, so when she announced something like that, there was no doubt she was being serious.

However, they could not sit and stare at each other all day. No matter what, they had to rescue Hyland—for Col's dreams, for Hyland himself, and for the sake of those awaiting God's teachings.

He breathed deeply and spoke.

"I'll hear it." He then added words that showed his pride as Myuri's older brother. "No matter how troubled I may be, I will figure something out."

Myuri's hair trembled in anticipation.

Before she said anything, he got the feeling she mouthed "stupid" to him.

"Once you save that blondie, you're going to become a priest, right?"

"Yes. You were angry about that before. What does that…Don't tell me."

Col came to a realization.

"Don't tell me this is because I might become an enemy of those considered possessed by demons once I become a priest?"

In the scripture, there were many stories of the prophets fighting against demons. But he must have explained to Myuri properly. No matter what happened, he would always be her friend.

"I'm not that inflexible. But if you think about how God created all things, then every living creature is a product of his—"

"No. That's not it at all. I don't care about that even a little. See…see…if you become a priest, then you won't be…"

Myuri got into a huff, her eyes watering, and her ears and tail suddenly appeared as she spoke.

"…You can't get…"

"What?"

"Married! You won't be able to get married!" she yelled, and everything in Col's mind was scattered to the wind.

"…Uh…What?" Overwhelmed by shock, he asked again. "Me?…To who?"

He could not find the words to accurately describe Myuri's expression.

She probably had no idea what to do.

Myuri was the first to calm down. She peeped through the latticed door before rubbing her hands on her face, frowning at the heat from the friction before she continued talking.

"See, that's why I didn't want to say anything!"

This time, she did not hold her head, but instead hugged her knees, looking away in a huff. Her lips were pouting and her cheeks puffing up, while her tail thumped against the floor. Col realized that though sometimes her face turned bright red from

205

anger, this time it was doing so because she was embarrassed. Also, he was a complete fool.

"Um…"

"What?"

He was heating up like a stone in the furnace.

He needed to say something, but he did not have the slightest idea what.

"R-rea…No, um, since…when?"

Instinct told him that if he asked "*Really?*" then she might tear out his windpipe.

He changed up his question at the last moment.

"…I don't know."

He had a feeling she was mumbling, "How should I know, stupid?" against her knees.

Of course, Col was aware that Myuri clung to him. She was so attached to him that it sometimes made her father, Lawrence, complain. Col thought she was cute when she did so, and he of course held her dear. But he had never looked at her in a romantic fashion.

But when he thought about it, many things fell into place. How she played around with his vow of abstinence, how she teased him, how she willfully hid in that smelly barrel and showed him an outfit she had specifically prepared, and her incredible insistence on following him along for the journey—everything suddenly made sense. Therefore, she had to see Hyland as an enemy. Hyland came from the outside world and would take him to a faraway land.

Then, it would be just as she had warned him. Considering the nature of his dreams, he would never be able to respond to Myuri's feelings. At the same time, he did not want to hurt her. Col found himself trapped between these two truths, unable to move.

He was embarrassed for his grand speech about justice and whatnot. If a personal problem arose before him, he could not dismiss it as a trivial matter. He understood how Myuri stood up to Hyland's justice with her love alone. It balanced out quite well.

Now the problem was how the balanced scales would tip, and even Col did not have a clue as to the answer. There were metaphysical questions in theology that were grossly overwhelming, such as how many angels could dance on the tip of a needle. But commonplace questions regarding who loved whom were even more difficult. Myuri's indication that Col was only looking at half of half of the world was scarily accurate.

But even though he knew the truth now, there was nothing to be done. All he could think of was to tell her how pitiful he was and that she deserved to find an even more wonderful person.

Even he knew how miserable that would be.

And then, as though she had seen straight through to the agony in his heart, Myuri gave off a loud sigh.

A girl half his age glared at him out of the corner of her eyes.

"It doesn't matter. I know you just think I'm like an ermine, running around in the hills and fields."

She was cute and nimble. Ermines certainly had particular characteristics, like sneaking into food storage sheds searching for this and that, that resembled Myuri's.

"But if I hadn't told you now, I don't think you'd ever notice, so I guess it's okay. Once you save the blondie, you'll leave me behind and go to the Kingdom of Winfiel anyway, right? Because it'll be dangerous once the fighting starts or whatever."

Myuri firmly stroked her head to hide her ears, putting away her tail, and stood up.

There was no way to trick her. He could not logically consider taking her to the Kingdom of Winfiel. Once the war started, the strait would be blockaded, and he could not imagine what horrific tragedies awaited them if they lost.

"You're…right."

The intelligent Myuri glanced at him sideways, then snorted.

"I liked you! Stupid."

She spoke in a way that sounded like her age, and it was cute.

"So? What's happening again?"

Myuri could change tacks quickly if she slept well. Or perhaps she simply understood that nothing would come of anything if they stayed standing here. Much like how he knew her from when she was a baby, she had been looking up to Col ever since she was born.

But he felt like a very thin film had formed between them.

Col felt like that fine barrier was cutting off her voice, her actions, even her warmth—everything that was precious to him.

It would be selfish of him to feel sad.

Life was a journey, and journeys were a series of meetings and partings.

"Um…According to Heir Hyland, Mr. Stefan from the Debau Company was going to come collect us. Then, we must negotiate."

"How confident are you?" she asked coolly, but Col preferred that to her clinging to him with hot tears streaming down her face.

"Not at all. The Debau Company is an organization of merchants. If we don't have anything to offer them, they may not heed our proposals."

"Why not tell them to save blondie, and if they don't, we'll die?"

"That's the best I can think of, too, but is that possible? I've heard it's just a myth that you can die from biting your tongue."

He did not even have anything like a short sword.

"…I don't even want to do anything like that for blondie in the first place."

"I can easily imagine that Mr. Stefan will already know we want to save Heir Hyland. Even if we stubbornly insist, the most we'll manage is getting stuffed into sacks and taken back to Nyohhira. That way, Mr. Stefan can say he was fulfilling his obligations. We have to bring something, *something* to negotiate with."

The Debau Company was a profit-seeking organization. It was clear that there was no point in appealing to them with nothing but faith and conscience.

Conversely, he knew they would pay attention once the conversation became about concrete gains and losses. That was the only thing they were frank about.

However, Col of course did not have any worthwhile ideas or assets to barter.

He did not have any means.

"Oh God..."

He gripped the crest of the Church that hung from his neck and groaned. Myuri was staring at him blankly, but she would not insult God or faith right now.

He exhaled deeply again and was about to again examine anything and everything that came to mind.

"If we're just going to be saving the blondie, then I can manage that," Myuri said, still expressionless.

"And that's...?"

Myuri sighed, rustled around inside her shirt, and fished out a small pouch that was tied together with string.

It was the pouch stuffed with wheat that her mother, Holo, had given to her.

"Didn't I say that as long as I had this, I could help you whenever you needed it the most?"

"Don't tell me..."

Myuri's mother, Holo, was the avatar of a wolf who lived in the wheat, and she could freely change between her girl and giant

209

wolf forms. But Myuri should not have been able to transform into a wolf.

Col looked at her with eyes widened in surprise, and Myuri spoke with incredible distress on her face.

"I practiced really hard...so if I don't do it right, Mother will get really mad at me."

There were legends about lions that dropped their young into bottomless ravines.

Perhaps wolves were the same.

"But it's all because I want to protect you, Brother, and not to help that blondie. Okay? I'm doing this for your dreams. Because when people like you have their dreams destroyed, they get so depressed and end up wasting away. It's hard to watch. I don't want such a gloomy person in a village as small as Nyohhira. So I'd prefer it if you chased your dreams and had your stupid fun somewhere far away. Understand?"

Myuri was being overtly condescending, but her expression made it clear that she was saying these things more for herself. As a romantic herself, she probably did not want to use her trump card in a situation like this. There was no mistaking she had imagined using it in a different situation, one where they had been driven into desperate and dangerous straits, when the knight would rush in to fight the dragon that had captured the princess.

And even still, she had a tool in her hand that would open the door, and she was helping him, even though what lay beyond was an outcome she did not wish for.

Her affection for Col reached him through her actions.

Myuri's eyes filled with drive, as though she was enduring some trial. Col gazed into them and said, "I understand. Myuri. Really...truly, thank you."

More pain crossed her face, but she turned away in a huff.

"I don't mind…if you reconsider falling in love with me again, you know."

She glanced at him out of the corner of her eye, but he could not determine if she was serious or not. Perhaps it was both, and he had no choice but to take it as a joke.

"I have reconsidered. You are a very selfish person, but a nice, kind girl who can save people."

"Hey!"

She was obviously angry, but also sad. Still, her ears and tail did not show.

He could tell she had made a clear decision in her mind.

He had to do the same.

"But what will we do after we break everyone free and get out of the manor? Are we just going to run? I can't give people a ride like Mother can."

Apparently, Myuri could not transform into a giant wolf who could swallow people whole. The best option would be to escape to the Kingdom of Winfiel by sea, but it would be difficult to procure a boat. It took considerable manpower to operate a vessel hardy enough to cross the strait.

Beings such as demon possessed or sprites existed on this earth, but they had their reasons for trying their best to conform to the human world and living unnoticed. The society that humans created was a complicated one, and sheer brute force was helpless against much of it.

"I want to get to the Kingdom of Winfiel, preferably by boat."

"Then, should I give Sir…er…I mean that Stefan guy a little nip in the butt? I'm sure he can at least prepare a boat for us."

The errand boys at the company must have called Stefan "Sir."

"No…Even if we manage to coerce him to get a boat for us,

there is no way we will go unnoticed by the archbishop and the papal officer, and that won't do. Mr. Stefan is innocent, and if things go poorly, then the problems may affect the Debau Company itself. The wagon that brought us to this place is still here, so let's escape with that. We can get to the kingdom from any town, as long as Heir Hyland's connections are there. As for you, we'll send a letter to Nyohhira and ask Holo and Lawrence to come get you."

"…Okay. So right now, we just need to rescue blondie and friends, who are all being held here. The sun has set, so that's perfect."

Beyond the barred window, he could see the faint glow of the city center and the silhouettes of the tall buildings against it.

"Let's go."

"Okay."

Myuri opened the little pouch she had received from Holo, retrieved some of the wheat inside, and put it in her mouth.

She swallowed it like a bitter pill and suddenly looked at Col.

"Brother."

"What is it?"

"…Look away."

Myuri seemed embarrassed. Though she did not seem to mind him seeing her naked, apparently watching her turn into a beast was another story. Col had no reason to refuse, so he turned his back and virtuously covered his eyes.

Then, he recalled that she was still wearing borrowed clothes and whirled back around, but the silver wolf was already before him.

"…*I didn't tell you to turn around. I wanted to do some grooming first…*"

Myuri was always self-conscious about her appearance, and

her red eyes bored into him. She was certainly smaller than Holo, but she still dwarfed the wolves normally found running about the forest. If she stood on her hind legs, Myuri would easily be taller than him.

"...I was just about to remind you that you were still wearing your clothes."

"They ripped, didn't they?"

Fragments of cloth were strewn about her.

The pouch from Holo was also on the floor, so he picked it up and placed it in his shirt.

"But I'm glad you're not scared, Brother."

"I've seen Holo's wolf form many times."

"I know. She said you really liked her tail."

He found embarrassment creeping over him, and he cleared his throat.

"And priests do not fear wolves. The ancient saint Hiero calmed the rampage of a ferocious wolf by removing the thorns stuck in its feet, and he then became the patron saint of livestock and hunting. He is always depicted with a wolf in art."

"That argumentative tendency of yours is your biggest flaw."

Her tail whacked him in the face.

"What should we do about the clothes I left at the company?"

"Cough...your clothes? I'll send a letter later for those."

"Well, that's fine. It's not like I have anyone to show them to anymore."

She regarded him spitefully, and he could only shrink back.

"It's a joke. It's not your fault."

Then whose fault was it?

As he wondered if he should retort with that question, Myuri shivered.

Then, she bit into the latticed door to distract herself.

"Grrrrr..."

Accompanying her distinct, earth-rumbling growl was the creak of wood, and she crushed the latticed door like soft cheese.

"Peh!"

She shook her head at last, and with a series of *cracks*, the hinge burst off the latticed door. Myuri removed the fragments of wood stuck in her mouth with her front paws and glanced back at Col.

"Aren't you going to praise me?"

"Well done."

"That's all?" she said. Her large frame crept toward him, and she rubbed the rigid nape of her neck. Apparently, this was a demand that he pet her. Her form was a frightening wolf, but on the inside, she was still Myuri. And though she was large, she was still a realistic size, so nothing prevented him from bringing her around town. For a moment, he imagined Myuri waiting by his side as he preached, scripture in one hand.

He rubbed at her fur as if to erase the image.

"What a beautiful coat."

He spoke absently, and Myuri's red eyes turned to him, her teeth on display.

He could tell she was smiling contentedly.

"Take care of the rest."

"Leave it to me."

Her tail flicked to the side, and despite her great size, she slipped out into the hall without a sound. The hallway was dark now that the sun had set, creating an especially surreal scene.

Myuri sniffed the floor and set out without any hesitation.

Suddenly, she broke into a run around the corner ahead, and Col immediately heard a yell.

It became quiet again soon after, and Myuri returned with a key ring in her mouth.

"...And the guard?"

"Delicious."

His eyes unwittingly darted her mouth to check if there was blood.

"I licked his face the moment we ran into each other. I think he heard the noise and was coming to investigate."

Even the hardiest of mercenaries would faint at a sudden encounter with a wolf's tongue in the darkness.

"Most of the soldiers are gone from the manor. I wonder where they went."

She lifted her head, and her great nose sniffed the air.

"I think the blondie's room is upstairs."

When she did not say "downstairs," relief washed over him. He had imagined torture occurring in the basement.

"Then let's go."

Quietly, quickly, Col followed after Myuri as she proceeded with her head low. He wondered if their audacious progression would be all right, but the halls were empty and the whole manor was quiet. When she ascended the stairs, he could hear muffled cries and groaning coming from above, but then they fell silent. After he reached the top, soldiers lay collapsed on the floor, their eyes blank. A handheld candlestick holding a still-burning candle lay on its side nearby, so Col picked up the light source and took it with him.

Myuri was already at the end of the hall, sitting motionlessly in front of one room.

When he cast the light on her, she resembled a statue even more.

—Is this it?

He whispered and pointed to the door. She raised her tail once, then quickly lowered it as confirmation. He placed his ear on the door, and he could hear voices inside. Perhaps Hyland was being interrogated at that very moment.

215

"When I knock on the door, I want you to get them when they come out."

In lieu of an answer, she rose to all fours and leaned forward, ready to pounce at any time. Then, just before he knocked, he suddenly froze. Myuri sent him a questioning gaze.

"Heir Hyland might be surprised, seeing you like this."

She waited for his next whispered words.

"But I will most definitely defend your honor."

Her red eyes slowly closed, and she resumed her previous stance.

He took a deep breath and rapped his knuckles on the door.

"We've received news! It's urgent!"

He knocked again, feigning urgency. For a few moments, he could sense their hesitation on the other side of the door, and after another knock, he heard someone rise from a chair. Then, the moment the bar on the door was lifted, Col and Myuri forced their way in with all their strength.

"!!"

Everything happened in an instant. By the time Col saw Myuri slip into the room like so much smoke, she was already pinning the soldier down with her paw.

"Heir Hyland."

He passed by Myuri to enter the room, and Hyland finally recovered from the shock.

"C-Col?"

"I'm glad you're safe. We've come to rescue you."

The room was bleak, with only a simple table in the center of it. Hyland was not even tied up, and a single flask and two cups rested on the table.

"Am I hallucinating?"

Myuri sat obediently beside the door. The candlelight cast stark shadows that gave her the appearance of a delicate painting.

"God has graciously allowed me to make use of this animal."

To be fair, it was the truth. Hyland nodded in understanding, though he seemed confused still as he rose from the chair. But he was a valiant and intelligent person. Once his surprise settled and he studied Myuri without faltering, something caught his attention.

"Those red eyes..."

A chill came over Col, but Hyland shook his head.

"No, I won't ask. Our Kingdom of Winfiel was also led by a golden sheep when it was established."

In the Kingdom of Winfiel, where sheep were abundant, there was a legend of a giant sheep covered in golden wool.

If Col told Hyland that they had met that sheep once on a journey, he would laugh.

"And I was raised among scoundrels. I can tell most things by others' eyes."

Hyland bravely approached Myuri and extended his hand.

"You have good eyes."

Myuri lowered her head, slightly embarrassed, and allowed Hyland to pet her fur.

"Well then, I have been saved by a miracle. God is ordering me to complete my mission."

"I have the keys. Let us retrieve your companions and escape this town. Then, we'll prepare a boat at another..."

Col stopped mid-sentence and closed his mouth because of Hyland's countenance.

There was no joy at the occurrence of a miracle or the prospect of escape.

His face was instead painted in heroic resolve.

"I cannot leave this town. Run with my subordinates, Col. They're all good people who have dedicated themselves to my house."

"That's, ah…Heir Hyland, why?"

"On your way to this room, did you come across any guards?"

The sudden question startled him, as perhaps Hyland had information that they did not.

"There are no guards in the manor because they're all headed to the city center. The people from the Debau Company haven't come yet, either, have they? That's because they don't have the time to be rescuing us. Everyone gathering there was ordered to surrender the names of the Kingdom of Winfiel's sympathizers, for the sake of the townspeople."

Col glanced back at Myuri, and she eyed the unconscious guard by the door.

"It seems there are a great number of Church critics turning up at the town square with the translated scripture. The craftsmen and commercial associations I convinced seem to have risen up right on schedule. Several of them used rather unpleasant methods to stoke the flames of the craftsmen's passions before tonight, but that bright, red fire you see now is an inferno of anger."

They noticed it from the room. The town atop the hill was boldly burning.

At the same time, Col was relieved that Hyland did not plan the sacrilegious act of dressing a dog in priests' clothing. There was no error in his judgment. Hyland stood above those people—he followed the path of righteousness.

"The townspeople are greater in number, so they should have the advantage at the beginning. However, the instigators of an uproar born of energy alone cannot win against disciplined soldiers. They will reach a standstill, and once they understand that it will not develop into anything significant, they will run out of momentum. Many times, I have seen peasants and day workers quit in the middle of a revolt because they have work the next day. If the soldiers intervene the moment the tension relaxes, it will all collapse in a matter of seconds. A few people will be arrested as a warning, and tomorrow they will be hung on the street corner. That is how it always happens."

Hyland was a noble and a landowner. He knew much about popular uprisings and how they ended.

"Alcohol and atmosphere will spur on most of them, but a not insignificant number will be truly protesting. 'We speak for justice. The people earnestly seek an honest and pure God they can believe in.' But once the commotion dies down and they see their neighbors rotting away in the gallows on the corner, they'll think, *Hyland didn't come. No one from the Kingdom of Winfiel came.*"

And then, life would continue as always. Nothing would change in the days to come as the results of evil practices trickled down to them.

"People likely still believe I'm in the church, debating away with the archbishop. They will raise their fists to aid me. If they learn that I am not there, that I ran away a long time ago, who on earth would listen to me anymore?"

"But—"

"Listen, if I go, then the archbishop and papal officer can say that I stirred up the people. I'm sure the archbishop will want to do his utmost to avoid severe action against the townspeople. I'm sure he wishes to stay a prominent figure in town. That is why I…"

Hyland made his declaration.

"I have to go there and denounce the archbishop. I have to show that I am the leader of this upheaval. Sorry to have you go through all the trouble of saving me, but…"

He finished his speech as if in jest. Of course, it was no laughing matter.

"...Afterward, they'll kill me."

The pope had already sanctioned him as a heretic and declared war. Once Hyland stood at the head of the people, there would be no more room for vague decisions. Would the archbishop meet his demands and stand with them against the pope? If not, he would kill Hyland, announcing to the world that the pope will not give in.

Once Hyland appeared, the people's anger would not cool until it reached its conclusion.

"You don't think I can win by persuasion?"

Hyland was smiling, but Col was unable to respond. The young man could only shake his head. He prayed that the noble's resolute actions and convictions would reach someone who would accept them.

"Of course, now that the papal officer is here, I would appreciate one or two more supporters, but...Well, at this rate, it's much better than being tortured and made to suffer. At the very least, I want to be able to decide when my life should end. Afterward, even though all my brothers are terrible people, I know they'll make good use of the opportunity. No doubt they will make good use of my death for a theatrical display of sadness and mourning," he warned lifelessly. When Col imagined what kind of life Hyland had led, his emotions upon opening the scripture, his heart ached.

Then, Hyland saw his expression and a warm, happy smile crossed his face.

"Well then, let's get things moving. Some people should already be declaring that I've run away by now."

"Then, I, too—"

Col subconsciously leaned forward as he spoke, but Hyland reached out with a long arm and pushed his chest.

It was so sudden, Col stumbled and toppled backward into soft and strong fur.

Myuri broke his fall and growled up at Hyland over his shoulder.

"Did you hear God's messenger? I can go."

Myuri's large ruby eyes were fixed on Col.

"Even if you did come along with that wolf, it would only fan the flames of the commotion. Next time, knocking out a guard like you've done now won't be enough to settle matters. You need to be prepared to kill and be killed. And even still, it is up to fate as to whether or not you can protect yourself. I do not wish for you to be bloodied, Col. I could not stand to see that beautiful fur stained, either," he said.

Myuri said nothing and simply regarded Hyland quietly.

He was painfully aware that she did not want to hear anything from him.

Then, Hyland gave Col a troubled smile.

"Col, sorry for troubling you."

"No, don't be...O-oh yes, now we can ask Mr. Stefan from the Debau Company to help you—"

"Col."

He sounded like Col did when he was admonishing Myuri.

"Unfortunately, Stefan and the Debau Company are on the archbishop's side. That man sleeping there told me that the reason the archbishop knew about the sanction order ahead of time was because a Debau Company express ship leaked that information. 'So don't expect any help,' he said."

Col recalled the dragonfly-like boat that Myuri had told him about yesterday. She'd said it forced itself into the port as the sun was setting, which caused problems for the people working there.

"Stefan probably has some sort of secret agreement with the archbishop and enjoys special privileges. There has to be an economic reason as to why he's cooperating with the clergy even though most of the townspeople are against them. So I can't imagine him helping us. Rather, I would not be surprised if he's sent all his underlings out to every association head in order to pressure them into calming the situation—'*Your official stance will be in support of the Church, and if you do not listen, then we will no longer do business with you.*' The craftsmen are vulnerable to such threats. They will absolutely ensure that you do not escape. Oh, and don't try anything stupid. They know where you come from. One wrong move and disaster might befall Nyohhira. You don't want that, do you?"

"..."

Hyland finished his explanation and took a deep breath, then smiled at Myuri.

"Take care of this genuine servant of God. You don't see them much nowadays."

"*Woof.*"

Myuri howled just like a wolf, and Hyland seemed pleased.

"I thank God for the good fortune I had in meeting you."

It was a carefree, gentle smile.

They could not exactly show Myuri to other humans, so Col and Hyland shared the task of freeing their companion attendants from around the manor. Once they were all assembled, Col recognized again how few they were.

Though Hyland was not the type to go around with a large

retinue anyway, there were very few he could trust in the first place.

They wished to accompany Hyland to his fate as well, but he refused. He seemed unwilling to bring anybody but his few personal guards. They, too, knew that nothing they could say would reach him.

The wagon that had brought them here was still in the stable, and though it was a bit small, everyone could fit inside if they also used the driver's seat. The person driving would borrow the uniform of the unconscious, tied-up soldier and disguise himself. That way, they would most likely not be questioned when they tried to enter the city at such a time. Myuri had already left for the city walls, however, and was probably already trouncing the watch around now.

The center of the town upon the hill was glowing a deeper and deeper crimson.

It was said that candles burned the brightest just before they were extinguished. There was no time.

"Well, Heir Hyland…Till we meet again…"

"Yes, I look forward to it."

Hyland stood before the stables, seeing off the wagon carrying his subordinates with a smile.

Then, he untied a horse and brought it to the entrance of the manor.

"You go, too."

It pained Col that he had no reason to say no.

"The translation of the scripture should be in your head. Do all you can to antagonize the pope and friends."

As long as he had pen and ink, he could re-create the translation many times. He could carry on Hyland's will.

"Well, then."

Hyland gripped Col's hand and forced the reins into it, then spun on his heel. He exchanged a few words with his personal guards, who were disguised as soldiers, and then jumped up onto a horse, alone. He did not look back at them. He kicked its side and set off with the guards.

Hyland left nothing behind and simply disappeared down the road.

It was his last act of consideration, ensuring Col would not reel from his departure.

"Brother."

Suddenly, a silver wolf appeared from the shadows, and the spooked horse tried to run. Col tugged on the reins, and it calmed.

Myuri had returned from her mission at the city wall, and she rubbed her big nose and neck on his face. When he did not move, she spoke slowly.

"Let's go home."

He looked at her, and she returned his gaze gloomily.

Her red eyes were telling him there was no way to save Hyland.

Would God not reach out to such a dedicated servant?

"Why am I…so powerless?"

He gripped the Church's crest on his chest so hard it might meld with his hand and fought back the tears. He only had his knowledge on paper—he did not have powers like Myuri; he was not noble like Hyland; nor did he possess the talents of the great adventurers he had once accompanied, Lawrence and Holo.

He was nothing but a lone dreamer fantasizing about an idealistic world.

"Why…why…?"

It was when the sob slipped from his mouth.

A sudden impact connected with his stomach, and the earth and the skies reversed.

It was so sudden he did not feel any pain, and when he opened his eyes, his vision was filled with rows of sharp teeth.

"Do you want to be God?"

Myuri was looking down at him, her eyes watering with tears.

"Hyland thanked you properly and praised you so much even though you seemed uncomfortable. That praise was real. They'd sometimes come and listen when you were so absorbed in working. That's why Hyland said he needed to work hard, too, and that it was God's will that you met."

He had no idea.

"That's why, Brother, I did everything you told me to. You brought support to someone who couldn't find any in this world. Doesn't that make for a splendid priest?"

This was the first time she had called Hyland by his proper name, and she poked his cheek with her nose. It was as though she was trying to force her words into his head.

"And you're not the powerless one, Brother. Mother told me something once. She said, even with big fangs and claws, there are many things you can do nothing about. So find someone precious. And I did."

Her left paw heavily pushed down on his chest.

"Guh?!"

"And that someone said no."

She was pressing so hard upon his chest, he genuinely could not breathe. He gripped her front leg, and she finally removed it.

"Nyohhira is not as complicated as the outside world, and there's nice hot water."

It was a rather convincing claim from Myuri since she was born and raised there.

"Brother."

The last word was not spoken kindly.

He knew that if he did not respond, it would hurt her. A man who turned down a wonderful girl like Myuri at the very least must grow into a worthy person himself.

He got up and brushed the dirt off his clothes. When he did, Col finally noticed that the string on the crest in his grip had been torn off.

"..."

He felt Myuri's gaze on him and smiled dryly.

"I will not throw it away."

"Oh, too bad."

If Col cast off the teachings of God, then he would no longer have a reason to uphold his vows of abstinence.

That being said, if he tossed the crest of the Church away, then Myuri might get angry or sad.

"Let's go back. I have the obligation to protect you and take you back to Nyohhira safely."

"Ooh, you're going to protect me?"

Myuri contentedly sniffed his waist with her big nose.

As he dodged her, he searched around in his clothes and took out his wallet to put the crest away.

"I feel like I'll be punished for putting it with my coins..."

"No, you wouldn't. I think they'd be happy."

"Why would you say such a...?"

"What? But isn't the Church collecting a lot of money? I went into the church to help, and the donation box was stuffed with change. There was even a picture of an angel with a scale at the company, too."

When he met with the Debau Company messenger, he had even said something about the scripture in one hand and the scales in another. Perhaps it was a theme that the people of the Debau Company particularly liked.

"I told you before that the scales represent equality. The sword is justice."

"*Really? I thought it was equipment meant for squeezing tax money out of the townspeople.*"

The sword threatens, and the scale weighs the coins. He thought her statement was rather disrespectful, but it troubled him that he understood where she was coming from. A single painting could inspire many interpretations.

And of course, it would not look good for the Church if their donation box was constantly packed with coins. But the clergy would use that money for charity and other holy works in the community. They should be recirculating that money back into the town. That was why appearances alone were not enough to judge...and his thought process stopped as something occurred to him.

Recirculating the money back into town?

He felt like he had heard something that contradicted that claim somewhere.

"*Brother?*"

He must have stopped in his tracks deliberating again, but Myuri's voice pulled him back to the present.

And then, he remembered. The scales.

"The money changers..."

"*Huh?*"

When he became aware of one thing, a long chain of ideas fell into place. The reason he left Nyohhira in the first place was because he could not accept how grubby the pope was with money.

His vision blurred, and when he came to, Myuri was supporting him.

"*Brother? Sorry, did I hit you somewhere?*"

Her side was holding him up, and her neck and tail hugged him worriedly on either side.

But he could not respond right away. His thoughts were roiling inside his head, and he could not breathe.

"Donations…The angel and the scales…The Debau…Company…"

The picture in his head was coming into focus.

The Debau Company and the Church were connected by mutual benefit, and that was why the company supported the Church. What would happen if such an exchange became a scandal? Even if it was originally nothing more than a simple transaction, it could be interpreted differently depending on how the fact was presented. Like Myuri said, even a painting of an angel could look like a greedy demon.

If they suggested such a thing to Stefan, his face would undoubtedly go pale. Considering the current situation and environment, the townspeople would direct their anger at the Debau Company, it would lose many of its business dealings, and most importantly, would likely be torched by the mob. Despite all that, would the company still wish to support the archbishop?

After removing the Debau Company's support, the archbishop would probably also crumble. Even with the papal officer's sanctions, parchment could not defend against the sword. Plus, it was a terribly long distance between here and the pope's seat of power. If the pope could not come rescue the archbishop by the time he hung at the gallows, then his authority meant nothing.

The painting of the angel with the sword and scales gained a third meaning.

Life or profit.

They had to try.

Hyland had told them to abandon him, but they could not. It was much worse for priests to give up than it was for merchants, because they were people who devoted their entire lives to asceticism without complaint in order to encounter a God that no one had ever met.

"Brother."

Myuri called his name, and he turned his attention to her; her red eyes were narrowed in exasperation.

"You look scary."

"I was just thinking."

"I like your angry look. And when you're flustered, too."

It was even more embarrassing to hear it coming from a wolf. That was when something came to mind.

"Myuri, you weren't trying to make me angry on purpose, were you?"

Myuri just whapped the back of his head with her tail and did not answer.

"Honestly…But it seems that selfishness of yours comes in handy sometimes."

"Really?"

"If we hadn't gone shopping for food, I'm sure I would never have noticed. I see…Guess I should get my nose out of my books sometimes and walk about town."

When he saw her blank stare, he considered how expressive the faces of wolves could be.

"And everything you saw and heard about town. Two heads are truly better than one on a journey. Especially if I'm only looking at half of half of the world."

He stood and said, "There is still something we can do to save Hyland. We can still fight for our ideals."

"Aww…"

Though she complained, her fur bristled enough to make the horse look away in discomfort.

229

"There is no time. You said you cannot carry people like Holo can, but is that true?"

Myuri's eyes crinkled in a grin.

The cold air sliced his ears like knives. On the other hand, the parts of him touching the rough fur below him became so hot that they were sweaty. Col clung to Myuri's back as she zipped through the rural countryside in no time before jumping into a desolate residential area without losing speed at all. With unbelievable tenacity, she leaped over crates, strays, laundry, work wagons, and every other barrier along the roads. Whenever they turned a corner, she made a great leap, which felt like they were running on the walls sometimes, but he did not think too deeply about it. He believed that Myuri would be all right.

When she finally slowed down, they were about a block away from the Debau Company trading house. A great tumult echoed around them like thunder and lightning. He wondered if Hyland was all right amid the chaos of the town square.

When Col alighted from Myuri's back, she opened her mouth wide, and the steam that left it was whiter than that of the hot springs.

"Are you all right?"

"I want to keep running."

"...The distance between here and Nyohhira should be just about right."

There was considerable strength in the angry flash of her fangs.

"Find a place to hide yourself around here."

"Aww..."

Of course, that was not a straightforward response. Her red eyes pierced through him coolly, as though saying, *Why would you say that?*

"It's a joke."

Myuri jabbed him with her nose.

"Brother, I don't like the way you're acting. What are you plotting?"

"Nothing. I've just thought of a way to make Mr. Stefan realize he's done something wrong."

"What are you going to do?"

When she asked, he flung back his cloak, which was unmistakably the vestment of a priest.

"You and Heir Hyland both taught me that you boldly declare something, then it will seem true."

"Huh?"

Myuri tilted her head, and Col whispered his plan to her.

She suddenly bared her fangs and wagged her tail.

"What do you think?"

"I think it's a perfect lie for an honest boy like you."

No, it was not a lie.

They would simply manipulate the other party into misunderstanding all on their own.

After he had this thought, Col suddenly wondered if Myuri was corrupting him, but it was not a bad feeling.

Col knocked on the back door of the Debau Company and was asked to identify himself.

"I am Tote Col, staying here as a guest."

The inspection window on the door opened, and a familiar face appeared. It was Lewis. He peeked out of the window with a grim expression, which instantly turned to relief. The commotion was happening nearby, so he was likely on the lookout for thieves taking advantage of the chaos or people with torches.

"Welcome back. I am glad to see that you are safe."

Lewis probably had no idea that they had just been arrested, been thrown in jail, and then escaped. He opened the door for them immediately.

Col entered, and just after Lewis bowed politely, he saw what came in after him and froze.

"Where is Mr. Stefan?" Col asked, but Lewis was frozen in a strange pose, and only his eyes turned to look at him. He seemed to believe that if he moved at all he would be swallowed whole.

"It's all right."

Col smiled softly and patted wolf Myuri's head. She gave a throaty growl, wagged her tail, and lowered her head like a dog.

The miraculous sight overwhelmed Lewis.

"H-he's in the office…"

"Thank you."

Col walked off after offering his gratitude, and Lewis sank to the floor.

"Am I that scary?"

She seemed rather hurt, but she jabbed him with her head as though telling him not to speak.

The large building was quiet throughout. Perhaps it seemed that way because of the chaos happening before their eyes and under their noses, or perhaps the company was holding its breath to hide its dealings with the Church.

"Well, here it is."

The hallway in front of the office had been crowded with people just the day before, but now it was empty. There were cavities on either side of the door holding stone candlesticks, and fancy beeswax candles illuminated the spaces.

Col took a deep breath and knocked on the door.

"Mr. Stefan."

However, there came no response. He looked to Myuri, and she sniffed. Apparently, he was inside.

"Mr. Stefan, it's me. Tote Col."

If Stefan was in communication with the archbishop, then he would know that Col should not be here. Col could feel the bewilderment and confusion seeping out from the other side of the door. When he was about to just force the door open, he heard a voice from inside.

"Come in."

It was a steady voice, fitting for someone who ran a trading house.

"Thank you."

He opened the door and entered.

A giant world map hung on one wall, and it was the same as the one in the room they stayed in. What was different was on the opposite wall; there were huge stacks of parchment as well as parchment rolls that had been simply left there. Written on them were most likely transactions for an enormous number and variety of goods and a dizzying assortment of privileges and permits. The scripture, penned to guide people to a good life, was not that thick by comparison, but the amount of words needed for a large company to stay profitable was unbelievably large.

Stefan sat at a large desk in the farthest corner of the room.

"No, it really is you...So the report that Heir Hyland showed up is also...Huh?"

He saw Myuri slip into the room beside Col and seemed even more startled than the errand boy had been.

"Do you believe in the miracles of God?" he said, standing with wolf Myuri. Stefan opened and closed his mouth, but no sound came out. Someone who should be in jail was standing in his office next to a giant wolf.

Could it be anything but a miracle?

"Please relax. I am not here to punish those who have turned their backs on the teachings of God."

It was unforgivable for the devout followers of God to tell lies.

That was why Col was not lying.

Myuri was simply baring her fangs and growling.

"However, I do wish to spread God's righteous teachings."

Directly after Col spoke, Stefan gave a retort.

"Th-the Kingdom of Winfiel has been deemed heretical! The translation of the scripture that you wrote has also been banned! It is quite obvious who is the most faithful to his teachings!"

He probably yelled because he was aware of his shamefulness.

"Do the townspeople know this?"

Stefan was at a loss for words for a moment, but he was a merchant. He struck back quickly.

"They do! That is why they are causing such a ruckus! Learn from the Kingdom of Winfiel, they say! I can't believe it! They have no idea what that means! They cannot understand the glory of the pope and the beauty of the Church!"

The words that Stefan shouted at them were empty, and it sounded like he was trying desperately to convince himself. Perhaps Stefan had taken a gamble. He learned about the sanction through the company's information network, abandoned Hyland, and chose to side firmly with the archbishop. But against expectations, the townspeople did not fear the pope's sanction.

Hyland had presumed correctly. The people had had enough of the Church's tyranny.

Yet it did not seem that Stefan would give up. He was praying that the archbishop would win and their relationship would continue unchanged.

"By the way, I heard that you and the archbishop are from the same town."

Stefan stopped his yelling and suddenly fell silent.

He was more astonished than he was when Myuri entered the room.

"You seem to have many deals with the Church."

"Th-that's…that's, so what? That's something that e-e-e-everyone in town knows."

It was almost humorous how much he trembled. He was not a fool. He must have imagined the possibility himself—the distinct chance that his deep ties with the Church would also draw him into the upheaval if the Church came under attack.

"Everyone may know, but have they seen it?"

"…S-seen? Seen what?"

Hyland was right when he told him to look up from books once in a while.

"This trading house is weighing the donations that the Church has collected. Maybe exporting them to towns that need the change, correct?"

That must have been why Myuri was counting coins.

"And perhaps coin collected as tithes?"

"Y-y-you are…what—?"

"Perhaps it was an appropriate trade. But if you truly think so, from the bottom of your heart, then how about it? Why not explain it to the townspeople?"

"Wha…?"

"Let them see if a row of crates, all packed with coins, falls in line with the Church's teachings on asceticism."

"Ah…"

"Even though the locals grow more desperate for coins they need for daily life, the Church is sending off such a large amount to other towns for nothing but personal gain. If the people learn that, why would they believe that the Church is their friend? To make matters worse, the archbishop already has a great reputation for indulging in extravagant meals."

It was the same as the translation of the scripture. Once anyone saw it with their own eyes, they would understand immediately.

"Moderation, Mr. Stefan. The Church will certainly lose many things. But they were taking too much in the first place. Many of the Church's actions cannot be fully justified. Mr. Stefan."

Col called the man's name again before clearing his throat.

"Have you read the translation of the scripture?"

A greasy drop of sweat dripped from Stefan's chin.

However, the head of this branch of the Debau Company was not wearing the expression of a man whose mind had frozen. He was desperately calculating. It was the same as when he obtained information about the coming sanction from the pope, making the same computations before he sold out Hyland. The situation had changed when they escaped from jail. And yet the final, conclusive factor Stefan required was indeed missing, and because of that, Hyland prepared himself for death.

That was why Col came here with Myuri, fully aware of the dangers.

"You may evaluate the gains as much as you wish, but…"

Maybe Myuri sensed the atmosphere since she stood tall on all fours.

He was terrible at keeping up appearances in front of women, but he was used to doing so before God.

He put on his show.

"Why do you think that someone like me is treated so kindly by the distinguished head of the Debau Company, pillar of the northlands?"

Stefan most likely thought that Col was nothing but a traveling priest he often saw in town. But beside him stood a silver wolf, and he had somehow even escaped from imprisonment.

From the perspective of someone unfamiliar with the details, one had to wonder why the head of the Debau Company supported the Kingdom of Winfiel and why he ordered Stefan to treat this young man kindly.

The walls of the company were decorated with images of angels holding swords and scales.

The teachings of God were not a deception.

"Mr. Stefan."

Stefan, a man almost twenty years Col's senior, was shocked into sitting up straight.

This must be how a person looked when facing their final judgment.

"You will talk to the archbishop, won't you?"

However, as he raised his head, he still hesitated. And then, Col realized—Stefan and the archbishop shared a hometown. Perhaps this was not a matter of profit and loss.

"We do not wish to eradicate the Church. And though there are many problems with the archbishop, I have heard that he is rather dedicated to his holy work. I'm sure he will continue working in his position here as he has been, and I'm sure the people will want that, too."

The man had cried at the happiness of baptisms and weddings. Hyland had not confirmed it, but it was probably not wrong. Stefan's drawn lips trembled, but he suddenly relaxed as if the invisible strings holding him up had been cut. For a moment, Col thought he had fainted.

"...I...understand."

In the end, it was the archbishop that Stefan was concerned about. Not even this merchant director thought solely about money, never bleeding or crying.

"Then quickly send someone or go yourself to talk to the archbishop. If the town soldiers end up harming Heir Hyland, then God will weep!"

Stefan stood up so fast from his chair he almost flew.

Then, he put such a distance between himself and Myuri that

he practically slid with his back against the wall, and as he passed through the door, Col did not forget to call out and add—

"Keep our existence a secret. God is always watching over us."

Stefan looked back, his expression on the verge of tears, and quickly nodded several times before dashing away from the room. The door was left ajar, and Col could hear him desperately calling out to somebody.

Should the major support of this town, Stefan, change his mind, surely the archbishop would have to listen.

And since the clergyman did reach his position through human society and not the teachings of God, then he should see this event as part of the new ways of the world.

But perhaps that was a little too hopeful.

The room fell silent again, but he could not help but feel uneasy.

"...Do you think it will be all right?"

Myuri's red eyes shifted from the door to Col.

"I'm more worried if you've actually turned into a demon or not, Brother."

That was her way of saying yes.

"But if you're worried, then why not go to the church? If worse comes to worst, I can eat them and then run away, probably."

He wanted to take her up on that, but Hyland would not like it, and it might not be actually possible.

Col had somehow managed to trick Stefan, but there was no time to explain Myuri's existence to the crowds. Hyland had been deemed a heretic, and their hands would be tied if he was seen escaping by the power of a terrifying wolf.

That was how Col decided to do what he could do.

"Let us pray."

The reason he was in this place at all was directly because of Hyland's noble will. A commoner had no choice but to respect that. Despite his somber emotions, Myuri did not respond and scratched her neck with her hind legs.

Such easygoing behavior reminded Col more of a dog than a wolf.

"More importantly, we should go get my clothes now while we can."

"Huh? Ah, of course."

Perhaps being calm and composed like Myuri was the correct answer, instead of anxiety and worry. He had done all he could do.

And then, confident there were no people around, Myuri walked down the hallways as unhesitatingly as always, slid up the stairs, and headed to their room.

The smell of ink and parchment greeted them, and though they had been in that room just that morning, it felt like they had returned after a very long time. At the end of a day, this kind of place suited him much better than the violence of the world, even if he saw only a quarter of it.

He smiled wryly and noticed that Myuri had plopped herself down in front of the clothes folded in the corner of the room.

"Is something wrong?"

"...Yeah."

Her tail lay flat on the floor, and she spoke without turning toward him.

"Maybe I should just throw them away."

"What?"

Her clothes were flashy, and to use the words of God, they were profligate. However, it was true that Myuri wore them well. Even still, he remembered that she had happily put her outfit together to show off to him. It was partially his fault that the view of her back seemed so sad.

"Oh, but it's not your fault, Brother." Over her shoulder, she

said, as though she had discerned his thoughts, *"It's not, I just… can't wear them, like this."*

"Huh?"

"When I showed you the wheat, I said it was for when we really needed it, right? There's a reason for that."

Myuri turned to face him, her front legs neatly placed together. Only her eyes were cast downward.

"I'm different from Mother. Mother has a hard time hiding her ears and tail, but it's easy for her to become a wolf. I'm the opposite. That's why this is only when we need it the most."

"No…"

Even if she could easily transform, she might not be able to turn back. He knew that was what she meant now, and the blood drained from his face.

Even if they returned to Nyohhira, she would not be able to stay in the bathhouse as a wolf. She would not be able to stay in any populated area.

How could she decide to do such a thing for his sake?!

"C-can't we…can't we do something about this?"

He ran to her, and the silver wolf narrowed her eyes in pain and lowered her head.

It was as though the more he suffered, the more she suffered as well.

"Don't make that face, Brother. I'm really glad I could have an adventure, like the ones Mother and Father told me about."

Those words wounded his heart. Myuri was a kind girl. She had not explained any of this and simply acted for his sake. He had been so involved in fulfilling his own dreams that he had paid no attention to her.

Even though Col did not reciprocate Myuri's feelings for him, she had sacrificed herself for him. All his apologies and self-hatred beforehand were just self-indulgent.

241

There were no words to express how he felt, and he could only wrap his arms around her neck.

"Brother…," Myuri murmured quietly. *"But you know, there is a way to turn back into a human."*

He lifted his head, and Myuri was gazing at him earnestly.

"What is it? Please tell me!"

"But I don't want to see you suffer anymore, Brother."

"Myuri! I can't imagine anything that could make me suffer more!"

Myuri closed her eyes and showed her teeth. It was a troubled smile.

"I'm glad you feel that way."

"Myuri!"

He called her name, and after a few moments of silence, her eyes opened and turned to him.

"Are you sure?"

"Of course." Myuri, still hesitant, dropped her gaze before slowly lifting it again. "Remember the promise I made to you."

Col was Myuri's friend. That was even more certain than any prayer to God.

Myuri had opened the door to an outcome that she did not want, all for him.

So now, it was Col's turn. He would do anything, no matter how much misery it would cause him.

Her red eyes were staring at him. They were the same as when she was little and came crying to him upon learning that she was different from other people.

Then, those ruby eyes closed, as though she was going to sleep.

"It happens a lot in stories."

"…Stories?"

"Yeah. Lots of old tales… You even said that in the story of your

242

village, there was a big frog long ago, right? There are stories that must have really happened long ago."

That was true. A perfect example was the story of Myuri's own mother, Holo.

"That's why...you know..."

She opened her eyes and gazed at the floor. She then looked up at him like a disheartened puppy.

"The prince is the one that breaks the spell on the princess, right?"

"That's..."

There was no way he did not know what she meant. Though it was a sacred act, it would violate his vows of abstinence.

Myuri immediately looked away.

"No, you have dreams to become a priest, Brother. I won't make you do it."

"Myuri."

He looked straight at her. Though she was covered in fur, and her mouth was big and filled with sharp teeth, she was still Myuri, the same girl he had known since birth.

If it could turn her back, then he did not mind how uncomfortable he was before God.

"You can change back that way?"

"...Yeah, but—"

"Very well."

"Brother?"

If he hesitated here, then Myuri would most likely never believe anything he said anymore. No—she might never believe anything anyone ever had to say in the future as well. He did not want to imagine a Myuri who distrusted others with a cold stare and declared, *"That's nothing but talk."* He did not want her to doubt that there were things worth believing in, things that were genuine in the world. These were the golden bonds that preserved the most wonderful parts of life.

I see; so this is what Hyland was thinking when he went to the church, prepared for death, Col thought. Actions must follow through on faith.

Myuri indicated she was ready.

"Brother...Thank you."

Even if the mouth full of teeth made him shy, Myuri was still Myuri. Nothing was different about his cute little sister.

Then, he put his hand on her snout and brought his face closer to it.

"Oh, wait, um, Brother...?"

"What is it?"

"Um...It's embarrassing, so can you close your eyes? And your hands make me nervous, so...can you let go?"

Myuri looked up at him with puppy eyes again, her ears and tail drooping. She was a girl of age.

When the fact occurred to him again, he suddenly became rather embarrassed himself.

Col cleared his throat, let go of her, and closed his eyes.

"Is this all right?"

"Yeah."

He did not care how far the seat of God was, as long as Myuri could return to her human form again and they could live in Nyohhira as they always had. And this did not break his vows of abstinence. It was something meant to save another, and he had not given in to lust. Besides, even the prophets had to kiss those possessed by demons on the forehead and hands to save them. So this was...Then Col's line of thinking halted with a question mark.

A kiss on the forehead or hand? Then was it at all necessary to give a kiss on the lips? There were certainly many stories in which a prince breaks the spell placed on a princess by giving her a kiss on the lips, but could Myuri's situation even be called a "curse"?

Something was odd. What had Myuri said in the first place?

There is a way to turn back into a person.

He recalled her exact words and suddenly realized—

She never said that was the way to solve it in stories!

"Ah—"

He opened his eyes, and there he saw Myuri already back in her human form. She did not want him to notice, so she was holding back her hair back and keeping her arms and legs away, sticking her face out in an odd pose.

Then their eyes met; she grinned slyly and flew at him. Col moved to the side. He could hear the *thud* of her head hitting the floor behind him.

"Owww…"

When he remembered back, after his eyes were closed, he had heard Myuri speaking in her normal voice.

And if she had been practicing transforming with Holo in the first place, then of course she would be able to change back.

"Aww, I missed."

She did not act bashfully, nor did she try to hide her nakedness. Col was unsure what he should be angry about first.

He just stood and spoke.

"Myuri!"

Myuri shrugged and hid her face with her arms, but he could see her smiling underneath.

"I only did the same thing you did earlier."

She did not lie but had simply let him interpret it the wrong way.

He could not counter a sound argument.

"Urgh…"

"But you weren't lying when you said you would always be my

friend. I'm going to cry," she said with a bright smile, and his anger faded.

Nothing made him happier than knowing she finally understood the meaning of his resolve.

"By the way, can you hear those cheers coming from the square?"

"Ah, what? Hey, Myuri!"

She stood, her familiar tail wagging as she rushed to the window and flung it open.

Her arms and legs lit up as the light of the square reached them.

"It looks like it went well, Brother! Ba—"

Col plopped his coat onto her head.

"Ears. Tail. And you are a girl—be more modest!"

Myuri poked her head out from under the coat and draped it over herself, annoyed.

He suddenly felt dizzy; perhaps he had gotten too angry or too tired from these past few days.

"Gosh, you're always so cross."

"And whose fault do you…?"

"Oh, it did go well! I can hear blondie's voice."

Not paying any mind to his scolding, she leaned out the window, ears pricked up.

But this excitement would be the end of it. Myuri would return to Nyohhira, and Col would go to the Kingdom of Winfiel with Hyland. It would not be a depressing parting, but on the contrary, a rather good one.

"Oh, hey, Brother, this means you can collect on a huge favor now!"

And she went as far as to say such a thing.

But there was no need for that. Hyland was a noble person. He was truly glad it went well.

"Hey, Brother…Brother?"

He was truly glad…

"Brother, come on, are you okay?"

Col had run out of energy, and he wavered, but Myuri held him up. She was a mischievous, tomboyish girl, but she was reliable when the time called for it.

As his consciousness faded, he was not anxious. He was comfortable, like he was soaking in the baths.

She was constantly indulging him, so he gave in. At least it was the end.

He thought about this as the faint smell of sulfur invited him, and the last of his tension eased in Myuri's arms.

EPILOGUE

Col had not slept for several days straight as he translated the scripture; once it was finished, he had experienced a stifling test of endurance at the church; they were thrown in jail but then immediately escaped; and right after that he had given the performance of a lifetime.

In the end, Myuri played the biggest prank on him, and as the blood rushed to his head, the success of Hyland's counterattack allowed him to relax. Even the sturdiest of leather straps would break after such rough treatment. But such a small thread did so easily.

After suffering through feverish dreams for a long while, he finally woke up, and he was surprised to learn it was the third morning after that night.

"I thought you weren't ever going to wake up."

Myuri sat beside the bed, moody and about to cry. He faintly remembered her taking care of him. He extended his hand from under the blanket and gripped her small one.

She seemed embarrassed but happy.

"Where's Heir Hyland?"

However, when Col asked, all expression left her face.

"I don't know. Oh, but more importantly, while you were

sleeping, I read the scripture, and you know? I found something really cool. And…and…do you want to hear it?"

Myuri began chatting happily, but Col instead scanned the room to see that no one else was there.

"No, more importantly, where is Heir Hyland?"

He wanted to know everything that had happened. He was glad they were safe, but he wanted to know about the papal officer. And not to mention that if war was still going to happen, this was not the time to relax.

"Sheesh, Brother!"

Myuri pulled on his hand, but then he heard the noisy sound of footsteps and voices coming from outside the room.

"Heir Hyland! You have not brushed your hair or eaten!"

"I don't care!"

He tried to get up when he heard Hyland's voice, but Myuri pushed him back down and pulled the covers up over his face.

"Myuri, what are you doing?"

"Don't look. You shouldn't look."

"Hah?"

As they bickered, he heard the door open.

"Col!" Hyland called out to him, and Col threw back the covers.

Then, as Hyland rushed to his side with a smile, he wondered if he was still dreaming.

"Oh, you're looking much better. Are you hungry? We can get anything from town. I cannot thank you enough!"

Hyland's hair was not done up, and he had rushed over half-dressed and just as unassuming as always.

An unadorned Hyland.

Or perhaps it was better to say an undisguised Hyland.

"Ah, I'm sorry for coming to see you like this. When I heard you'd woken up, I had to come see you."

He pulled back his beautiful long blond hair and smiled.

And then, Col noticed Hyland's chest.

"Brother, what are you looking at?"

Col tore his eyes away in surprise. Hyland seemed to finally catch on.

But all he—*she* showed him was a troubled smile.

"Don't tell me you never noticed?"

When they had spoken in Nyohhira, it was in a grotto bath, and those were more like steamy saunas than regular soaking baths. He did wonder why she had been covering herself so much, but he had assumed it to be a habit of people in high society.

Appearances were important.

And he had told Myuri himself that there were two choices of dress for traveling women: a nun or a boy.

"See, didn't I tell you? You don't pay attention to aaanything, Brother."

Hyland looked at Myuri, then back at Col.

"You…No, you're fine the way you are—a wonderful servant of God."

As Col wondered if he should take those words as a compliment or not, Hyland tactfully cleared her throat and changed the subject.

"More importantly, the town of Atiph has now decided to side with us. The archbishop gave in. He has not told us that he will be a reliable ally, but what is certain, at least, is that he will not interfere with the will of the townspeople."

"Really?!"

"Yes. As Stefan changed his mind, he must have thought it would be pointless to keep the papal officer and his parchment as an ally. And it seemed that it was truly a shock for the archbishop to see that the townspeople did not fear the pope's sanctions. The archbishop told the papal officer that he wished for additional support from the pope and sent him away. The official had no choice—had he stayed, his life would have been in danger. Then, the archbishop proclaimed that he would lend an ear to understand the people's anger. I don't know if he will keep his promise, but he must be taking it to heart. Stefan, who had been hanging around like a bat, is now behaving like a dog with his tail between his legs."

Her smile was surprisingly mischievous.

"Either way, this information will spread soon enough. But once that happens, I can imagine that the pope will begin acting seriously. It's not over yet."

"This is but the beginning."

"Yes. From here on, we will correct what has gone wrong."

As Col watched Hyland happily speak, he realized why he did not notice her gender before. When she spoke of her dreams, she was as innocent as a child. A young child, regardless of sex.

"And I wanted to tell you once you got better, but after this, we plan to go to another town. I want to take advantage of these circumstances and create allies with all the towns on the mainland that look out over the Kingdom of Winfiel."

She was already thinking about what would happen once war began.

"Of course, I wish to accompany you."

"Thank you, and—"

"*And* about that."

The only one who would so rudely cut off the words of someone like Hyland was none other than Myuri.

"I read the scripture while you were sleeping, Brother. And I asked a lot about priests. And I also asked this bl— Heir Hyland. She said there's no problem."

What is she talking about? Col looked between Myuri and Hyland.

Like an older sister watching her tomboyish younger sister, Hyland's smile was troubled yet delighted.

"I'm not going back to Nyohhira."

"Myuri, we already—"

He wanted to walk a holy path. He could not reciprocate Myuri's feelings. That was certain, and she accepted it.

But Myuri did not shrink back. Instead, she smiled mischievously.

"Moderation, Brother. Your favorite."

"Moderation?"

"Yep. I don't want to get in the way of your dreams. But the scripture didn't say anything about it."

"…About what?"

"Mm. Priests should not give in to worldly and physical desires. They must strive for moderation. But *it didn't forbid or say anything about worldly people fancying priests.*"

"…Ah?"

Hyland stood by the bed, chuckling.

Myuri pushed the translated scripture into his face.

"If you don't believe me, just read it. So you see, Brother, moderation."

Col was not sure what she meant by that.

Myuri folded her arms and spoke proudly.

"As long as you don't try anything with me, then it won't be a problem."

"…"

He was speechless. He was astounded by the existence of such an interpretation.

"Your faith is going to be tested, Brother."

Her smile was filled with confidence.

He possessed parchment on which the holy teachings of God were written.

What he lacked was his dignity as an older brother.

He placed the sheepskin with God's teachings over his face and closed his eyes. He was now a sheep wearing sheep's skin.

"Oh God…"

"You called?"

He could not respond even out of pride, nor would he ever be able to explain why he felt relieved.

Beyond his closed eyelids, a silver tail waved mischievously.

It was the sheep's fate to always keep a close watch on the wolf's tail.

AFTERWORD

Before falling asleep, take a book into your hand, open to any page, and see cute animals, then fall asleep in peace. I wanted a book like that, so I wrote it myself. This is Isuna Hasekura.

I'm mostly joking, but it was a lot of fun writing an energetic girl as a main character.

But even I was surprised at how I decided on how our heroine, Myuri, was going to be. Because when I wrote the first short story in *Spice & Wolf, Vol. 18: Spring Log*, which is from the previous series to this one and out the same month, I had not written her directly yet, and I had no idea what her setting would be. The moment I indirectly portrayed her through a letter from her and Col, that was when she started to take shape. It's hard to explain, but it felt like she was already there on the other side of the letter in the story.

There are many strange things is something I thought to myself as I started writing this book.

By the way, for those of you who have first encountered the world of *Spice & Wolf* with this novel, as this book is called *New Theory Spice & Wolf*, the main character Col appears in the middle of *Spice & Wolf* as a younger boy, and the heroine Myuri is the daughter of the two main characters in that series.

The world is the same, and the story takes place one generation later. It's been said many times, but this is a work that anyone who hasn't read the earlier series may enjoy as well. Still, do please read the previous one, too. I'm sure it will be much more interesting with that knowledge! And I am hoping to elaborate more on the world in a way that I could not in the original series. I am excited to do things I was not able to do. I hope you will accompany me!

And so I feel adventurous having started a new series, so I feel the need to write completely different stories, and like Myuri pulling a prank, I am scheming many things. If you see them out in the world somewhere, please smile for me.

Well then, I will see you in the next volume.

Isuna Hasekura

Congratulations on the publication of *Wolf & Parchment*...!
When I first heard that the unexpected daughter of Holo
and Lawrence and a grown-up Col were the main characters,
I was shocked. Those who have stuck with *Spice & Wolf* have
no choice but to respond to this pairing. No fair...! (Yay!)
While I look forward to the story of their travels as a reader
myself, I will do my best to help portray their charm!

Jyuu Ayakura

ongratulations on the sale of *Wolf & Parchment*!

It's unusual to see a story begin with mutual love (?), but Col is a young man who wishes be a priest…He cannot avoid the distress of being loved by such an angelic Myuri. What a trickster, at Hasekura…I cannot wait to see what happens next!

Keito
Koume

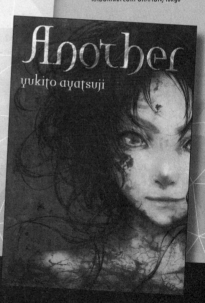